THE SPIDER:
THE SILVER DEATH RAIN

MASTER OF MEN!

THE SILVER DEATH RAIN

By Grant Stockbridge

POPULAR PUBLICATIONS • 2022

PUBLISHING HISTORY

"The Silver Death Rain" originally appeared in the March 1939 (Vol. 17, No. 2) issue of *The Spider* magazine. Copyright 2022 by Argosy Communications, Inc. All rights reserved.

CHAPTER 1
OUT OF THE NIGHT

T HERE ARE furtive, narrow streets in New York which the sun never warms and where, at night, the occasional lamps are smothered by close-pressing slattern walls. There are people here, but they slide from shadow to dark shadow and if they look at one another, it is with side-long, predatory eyes. In these places, even the police walk in pairs....

Such is Holian Alley which jogs its short and twisted length off the Bowery. It connects with nothing and leads nowhere, yet men enter there and do not come out. It is true that by ducking down a tenement basement steps and fumbling among the refuse heaps of the back courts it is possible to reach the malodorous gash of Almond Bloom lane. But there men of an alien race shuffle with their slant, inimical eyes upon the ground and the tourists never penetrate. Perhaps that is just as well....

Strange then that, near the mouth of Almond Bloom lane, a luxurious foreign limousine should pause, however briefly—and that a lithe man should spring from its back door to the shadows! The door closed soundlessly and the chauffeur did not even turn his turbaned head. The heavy machine trundled on, surged around a corner and, with a soft arpeggio from its harmonic-toned horn, vanished into the night.

From the shadows where the car had hesitated, a man presently slouched—a man in a battered shapeless hat, with broken shoes and a misfit suit whose bagginess concealed the lithe strength of his body and the resolute confidence of his broad shoulders.

Beneath the dog-eared hat-brim, his eyes were keen, and about the firmly chiseled mouth a slight smile played while the man bunched his shoulders to the cold bite of the wind that whimpered through Almond Bloom lane. A sign swayed, creaking in the erratic rhythm of the gusts. The street itself was soundless, deserted save for a single scurrying form that, even huddled in a heavy overcoat, showed the obsequious head-down shuffle of the Orient. But the man in the shadows waited until even that figure had disappeared before he slipped into a tenement entrance and found his sure way through the tumbled blackness of the back courts to a miserable room in Number One, Holian Alley.

SENSITIVE FINGERS now searched out a seal of chewing gum which guarded doors and windows and, by a brief flash of light, the man surveyed the fingerprint upon it—his own. So his room had not been entered! He nodded with satisfaction and, behind a drawn shade, he flashed on the lights and looked about him. Gone now the slouchiness of carriage, the furtive cringe to the shoulders. Here was a man among men, one born to command—that much was apparent at a glance. A smile that had its touch of recklessness moved his firm lips and he whistled almost soundlessly between his teeth... Tonight, the Spider would walk again!

A stride across the sloppy room took him to the bed with its heavy headboard and a touch on a secret spring there

revealed a complete make-up table with its special lights. He crouched before it, set to work on his face, changing it from the intelligent, cultured face of Richard Wentworth, clubman and dilettante of the arts, into the malformed and vicious countenance of Blinky McQuade, the half-blinded safecracker whom all the Underworld knew and accepted as a petty crook.

That same Underworld had been ominously quiet in recent months, and its very silence was significant to a man who, like Wentworth, had made its pulse his life-long concern.

The crowd fled in panic!

Driven by a double love of absolute justice and taut adventure, Wentworth long ago had dedicated himself to a battle against crime. But for months now he had been inactive. At first, it had been a welcome release from the constant turmoil of life-and-death battle. Now it grew irksome, and the reckless urge to adventure was working in him again....

Wentworth hummed to himself as he altered the lines of his face with skillful make-up.

The firm line of the mouth became loose and dissipated and a certain liquid sallowed his skin, drew it taut over the bones. A bit of putty then to malform the nose and a sandy, gray-shot wig, and he was almost ready. From the cache in the headboard of the bed, he drew out a pair of hooded spectacles, broken and mended with bits of string, which he hooked over his ears. They completely hid the keenness of his eyes—and they had given Blinky McQuade his nickname. He was supposed to have been almost blinded by the back-flash of a pete-blown safe....

Wentworth was ready then, but he stood for a moment in the middle of that slattern room, glancing about him with deliberate, keen eyes. He unfastened his vest and, close about his body, he fastened a girdle of silk whose vertical pockets contained a kit of carefully devised burglar tools. From a holster beneath his arm, he drew out a heavy, blue-steeled automatic. His sure fingers checked its mechanism, and the smile on his lips had tautened a little when he thrust it away again. None knew better than he the danger he could run! There was always the chance that someone might discover that Blinky McQuade and the Spider were one—and that discovery would mean death to Richard

Wentworth! No man had more often thwarted the sure plans of the Underworld; and no man had more thoroughly earned their vengeance. That was why, ever through the dark alleys and secret purlieus of the half-world, the whisper could always be heard:

"Death! Death to the Spider!"

So Richard Wentworth, using the fumbling, stooped stride of Blinky McQuade, fared presently out of Holian Alley, made his way along the Bowery into the broken tenement streets beyond and ducked into an unmarked, unlighted doorway to climb slattern steps. Strangely, the second floor hallway had a brilliant unshaded electric light. Before a door, in no way different from any of the others along that hallway, a man stood. Wentworth scowled at him but did not speak—which was the way of Blinky McQuade.

The man scowled back, "Scram, Blinky," he said harshly. "This ain't no place for you tonight."

Wentworth recognized the man as a small-time hood who had done strong-arm work in the rackets before this and aspired to be known as a killer—which he wasn't. He had even dubbed himself Killer Murdock. The underworld called him the Mug....

"Go to hell!" came Blinky's snarling answer. But behind those hooded glasses, Wentworth's eyes were sharp.

Murdock, the Mug, was hiding something in the palm of his right hand and, from the way he held it, he would show whatever he held when the door was opened. Wentworth's suspicions flared brightly. This was the hideout of Iron Mike, where only known criminals were admitted, but it had never before been necessary to show a pass to gain ingress… It was only a hint, but it added fuel to Wentworth's earlier guess that there must be a reason for the brooding quiet of the Underworld! This closing of ordinarily open doors was one of the first developments when a new power began to rise!

Wentworth stumped toward the Mug. "Any time I can't get in where you can go," he snarled. "Anytime…."

The door opened and the Mug turned his shoulder on Wentworth, thrusting out his open hand toward the man who stood on the threshold. Wentworth had a transient glimpse of a small metal figure that caught the glint of the light in the man's palm, the figure of a flying bird! Then the Mug was passed inside and Wentworth was facing the guardian of the door.

Wentworth grumbled, "Hello, Mike." He shuffled confidently forward—but the man put a heavy hand flat on his chest and shoved him backward.

"Back up, Blinky," the man called Mike said in a thin, high-pitched voice. "It is necessary for you to prove up!"

WENTWORTH FELL back before that thrust, a cringe coming into his shoulders, for Blinky McQuade was no fighter. He called himself an artist in cracking a safe, but that was all. His lips shrank back from discolored teeth as he blinked up at the giant of a man who blocked his entrance. Strange that Iron Mike himself should be on the door. Iron Mike didn't like to heave his three hundred pounds about, and his usually moon-like impassive face was screwed up now from the effort of thrusting Blinky back. It wasn't that Mike couldn't move swiftly and with tremendous efficiency, if he wished. There was power under that fat. He scowled, and the shock of iron-gray hair moved forward over his forehead like an ape's.

"I must insist that you prove up, Blinky," he protested in his piping, incongruous voice.

"What the hell is this?" Wentworth demanded in Blinky's harsh tones. "You ain't goin' to keep me out just because I ain't got no nickel-plated boid to show, are you?"

Iron Mike's face blanked out and the pig eyes in their slits of fat held a curious glitter. "You see too much, Blinky," he said softly, "for a man with bad eyes. Sometime you will see your grave, no?"

"Aw, Mike, I never meant no harm," Blinky whined. "I just want to come in and have a drink with the boys. See if I can't pick up a job, maybe. You know me, Mike. What if I ain't got no nickel-plated boid?"

Iron Mike's hand shot out with a swiftness strange in so huge a man, and the fingers curled with iron strength on Wentworth's lapels. "Some time, Blinky," he insisted gently again, "you will see too much—and perhaps talk too much! Yes, I think you would better come inside. And don't, my friend—" the fat-padded hand was shaking Blinky gently, irresistibly—"don't again mention the bird. You understand?"

"Sure, Mike. Oh, sure. I get you. I won't mention the… I won't mention it again!"

Wentworth was propelled violently through the door. He

brought up against a wall and his glasses were knocked askew upon his eyes. He made his hands tremble as he adjusted them, put a cringe in his shoulders as he slunk along a dim hallway to a room where a half-dozen tables were jammed together with broken chairs about them—where liquor was thrust over an unlicensed bar. Behind him, Iron Mike stood impassively inside the door, fat, short arms dangling in seeming helplessness at his sides. He was colossal, monumental, a frozen image of a fat man except for the glitter of his tiny eyes… They seemed to tear aside every atom of the disguise Wentworth wore as he slunk into a chair at a table near where the Mug was drinking.

The Mug turned and looked at him in surprise, then grinned, a little placatingly. "Geez, Blinky," he said. "I didn't know you was one of the Silver Falcon's men, too."

Wentworth snarled his reply, "You don't know nothing, Mug—not a damn thing."

He sat alone, his shoulders hunched over his drink, paying no attention to the hails of recognition that greeted him. Behind the screen of those hooded glasses, his eyes were everywhere, and surprise drew their puckered lids close together. Iron Mike had an aristocratic gathering here tonight, too high class for such a middle-grade bit house. Knife Hogan was a daylight bank robber, one of the royalty of the Underworld, and he had with him two men of the same ilk. There was Chopper Jackson with his kill-crazy, unwavering stare.

Wentworth's heart began to beat in long slow pulses, and it was hard to keep the smile off his lips. Well, he had guessed right once more. Hell was brewing in the Underworld, and he was in the midst of it. With such men as Knife Hogan and Chopper Jackson about, he should not lack for adventure! He could feel the cold prickle of watching eyes. He did not need to turn his head to realize that Iron Mike's venomous gaze rested on him.

Wentworth finally twisted about slowly, Blinky's lips now carrying a fawning smile… Iron Mike's moon face remained impassive. Had his keen eyes detected the presence of make-up? Wentworth wondered, with an accelerated beat of his heart. The Underworld would need no more proof than that to spring upon Blinky McQuade and tear him to bits….

WENTWORTH TURNED his attention to the men about him. More than once, he caught the silvery sheen of the "nickel-plated boid"—a silver falcon, wasn't it? A falcon with its wings half-spread, swooping on its prey… And it was the insignia of a new power rising in the Underworld, a new threat to the safety and happiness of the people whom the Spider served so loyally, asking not even the minor recompense of thanks.

Grimness crept along Wentworth's jaw, hardened his gray-blue eyes. For once, the Spider was at the *beginning*—and by all the gods, he would see that it was no more than that, a beginning! He would crush *this* criminal plot, before it was fairly hatched—find and destroy this Silver Falcon!

Wentworth rose and sidled to the bar, carefully pulled a single dirty bill off a thin roll and spread it on the bar. He said, ungraciously, "I'll buy a drink, Murdock."

The Mug laughed, his weak mouth stretched wide. "Geez, not you, Blinky! You wouldn't spend an extra quarter!"

Wentworth closed a deliberately dirtied hand on the bill,

turned away, but Murdock caught him by the arm. "Geez, can't you take a joke, Blinky? Sure, I'll drink with you! That's something to brag about, though. Blinky McQuade buyin' a drink! Geez!"

Wentworth was conscious of Iron Mike's eyes still following him, but, except for an occasional ingratiating smile, he pretended to ignore it. Dangerous ground he was treading, yes—but he needed information quickly. The Mug could be flattered into telling what he knew....

"Just one thing keeping me from the top of the heap," said Blinky McQuade. "Just one thing... I ain't never had the nerve to rub out any guy. I had a tough time making the grade with the Falcon, account of that. But you know... you don't think nothing of that. I'll bet the Falcon tipped you to the whole job."

The Mug tossed off his drink with a leer. "Sure. Sure," he agreed. "Now if you'd like me to put in a good word with the Falcon for you...."

It was laughably easy, but the Mug didn't know much—just that they had been summoned to Iron Mike's tonight. Either they'd get their assignments here or they'd be told where to meet the Falcon to obtain the information about the job that was to be pulled.

The Mug whispered, "The Falcon claims the Spider is afraid of him and is laying low. It sure looks like the truth, too. Ain't nobody seen the Spider in months."

"This Falcon—" and Blinky McQuade's voice was strangely dry—"is quite a boid, ain't he?"

10

The Mug lifted the third drink that Blinky had bought him. "I'll tell the cock-eyed world!" said the Mug.

Iron Mike's voice cut in just then at the Mug's elbow. "Yes, Murdock, I believe you would," he said gently. "I believe you would tell the entire world, if something weren't done to curb your tongue."

The Mug whirled about and his face was gray with sudden fear, but he didn't talk. He didn't have a chance. The lights blinked out in that room with the crisp finality of death and in that darkness there echoed, faint and far off, the rasping fierce cry of a hawk!

Without an instant's loss of time, Wentworth slipped to his knees there beside the bar and his heavy automatic raked into his hand. No one moved in all that black room and nothing touched him. Only that scream came closer and there was, abruptly, the smashing clatter, the thin tinkle of broken glass as a window crashed in. Wentworth could make out the grayness of the broken oblong… and there against it poised the replica of that tiny silver falcon which was the pass-symbol of these men. But it was huge as an eagle and its plumage glowed like phosphorus in the dark!

Wentworth's automatic centered on it, but he checked his finger even as it tightened on the trigger. Madness to fire at any such apparition! It was meaningless mummery. That was what he told himself, but there was a touch of cold across the nape of his neck as a harsh, incredible voice spoke from the thing.

"Death to all traitors," it pronounced. "There is a traitor here. Meet at the other aerie—in an hour. *Death to all traitors!*"

The figure vanished and again there came that scream, tearing, predatory, filling the entire chamber. Crazily, Wentworth thought he heard the swift rush of pinions. He crowded back against the front of the bar and his gun muzzle swiveled upward… But the blow did not strike him. It came from somewhere near at hand, in the air above him… a sodden, crunching thud and the gasp of a man's breath driven out of his lungs. Something warm and moist touched Wentworth's face and then a man's body hurtled to the floor!

Screams then in that darkness; screams and the trampling panic of terror-stricken flight. Wentworth's teeth were locked and the curses that sprang to his lips were bitter. No need to guess who had died in the darkness. The Mug who called himself Killer Murdock had talked too much! No need to guess either, whose fate would next be sealed! The lips of the man who had listened to Killer Murdock; the lips of Blinky McQuade must be sealed… by death!

CHAPTER 2
DEATH TO THE SPIDER!

FOR A space of heartbeats, Wentworth crouched motionless beside the bar and the body of the man the Falcon had slain. Then, with a swift gesture, he pocketed the hooded glasses of Blinky McQuade and sprang away toward the thick of the escaping press about the door. Impossible to know when the blow would fall, or where, but it was pointless to remain supinely waiting for it. The Spider had a better plan!

Men jostled him on every side. He heard the door ripped open but even the brilliant light there had been extinguished and there was nothing to guide their flight. Wentworth allowed himself to be thrust out the door with others and then he turned and seized the man beside him; gripped his captive's wrists in a vise-like hold and wrestled him away from the fugitive stream of criminals.

"You are a traitor!" Wentworth hissed, and contrived to get into his voice some of the rasp of the hawk's scream. "You shall now die! Death to all traitors!"

The man struggled frantically, but Wentworth forced him back into a corner. "If you are not a traitor," Wentworth said, "Prove it!"

The man broke into a babble of fear. "In my vest pocket," he whimpered. "The Falcon...."

"Pah! Murdock carried the Falcon!"

"I'll swear!" The man could scarcely speak for the terror that shook him. "Listen, question me...."

Wentworth's grimly compressed lips moved in a cold smile. "Very well," he said harshly. "Where is the other aerie? If you can answer that...."

That man could, and did, and with a grunted oath, Wentworth released him, sent him stumbling in among the men still pouring down the steps. Wentworth himself took the way upward and ran on swift, light feet. He now had the information the Spider needed. If he moved swiftly, he could still smash this incipient conspiracy. But it would be wiser if Blinky McQuade disappeared. He had to return now to that hideout, for it was his only present chance to assume the disguise of the Spider, which was essential to his plans. Once he had done that, Blinky McQuade could vanish as he had before....

At the head of the ladder that led to the roof, Wentworth paused for a moment, listening with tautly attuned senses. Then he thrust quietly up into the coldness of the night air. Somewhere up here were the men who had operated the falcon with which they had smashed the window of Iron Mike's bit house. But Wentworth had no business with them now. They could wait... until the Spider invaded the other aerie! Yes, that was the best plan. These underlings to whom the Falcon had boasted that the Spider was beaten, must see the Spider triumph... After that there would be nothing left of the conspiracy save fear.

Wentworth's lips were crisp with a cold smile as he raced across the tenement roofs and took a fire escape to the street a block away. The hooded glasses were back over his eyes again, and he moved furtively. The killers would be searching for him among the fugitives, not at this far point; but he would have to hurry. They might beat him to Holian Alley and that might be disastrous... Nothing moved in the shadows of that narrow, twisted way when the hunched figure of Blinky McQuade scuttled into it, but he checked, tautly listening, inside the doors of Number One. Nothing there either....

A frown knifed Wentworth's brows as he felt once more for his seal over the door. No, the enemy were not before him. He dodged inside and, from its hiding-place in the secret compartment of the bed, he snatched a bundle wrapped in newspapers, tied with pieced string. It was the kind of parcel Blinky

McQuade might be expected to carry—and it carried his death warrant if ever the police or the criminals with whom he associated should open it. It contained the robes of the Spider!

Wentworth waited for no more than that, for seconds might make the difference between life and death for him now. Back through the basement and finally into Almond Bloom Lane he made his way and he peered in through a dusty window at an antiquated clock. Eleven o'clock. It was three hours yet before he had bidden his trusty servitor, Ram Singh, return with the car. But there was another machine hidden near here in a rusty-doored private garage. He slid into it after a preliminary survey of the neighborhood and fought the stubborn motor to life. After that first cold stiffness, the engine purred almost silently, despite the shabby exterior of the car, and the smoothness with which it moved bespoke the power hidden under the rattling hood. Against his need, Wentworth had four such cars hidden away in various parts of the city and rarely used.

Usually, Wentworth operated from his own home, a fortified mansion built back of Sutton Place and walled in by every burglar-proof invention of modern science. There he lived amid the luxury that his great wealth could provide; and which he more often used to battle against crime than to waste upon the multiform pleasures of the rich. There his fiancée, Nita van Sloan, would be waiting for him when his night's foray against the Underworld should be concluded.

Alone among all womankind, she knew the Spider's dread secrets, as was fitting since her love and loyalty were beyond question. It was part of the compact of love between them, that he should never venture into danger without notifying her so that she could come and wait... Wentworth frowned at a fleeting urge to telephone her. She was his repository of information, his second line of defense in case something should befall him. But as yet nothing had happened. He knew that a power called the Silver Falcon had raised itself up, but what threat he constituted to the people still was hidden from Wentworth; that and the manner in which he would strike. When he had learned that, it would be time enough to phone Nita... So Wentworth thought. He was to regret that decision terribly....

Briefly, he thought of Nita, and then put her image from his brain. Deadly peril lay ahead, for all that the Spider's swoop upon the aerie of the Falcon would be totally unexpected. He must lay his plans....

SCARCELY A mile away across the canyons of the city, another such rich limousine as Wentworth's Hindu chauffeur drove, was nosing its sleek way through the after-theater traffic of Fifth Avenue. The man who occupied the tonneau with a fur-wrapped girl was huge to the point of crowding even that roomy seat, but there was about him no suspicion of fat. The lines of his face were hard-boned, smoothly planed; his gloved hands moved with a quick, lithe sense of power.

"I'm going to have to ask you to pardon me, my dear," he said pleasantly to the girl. "Francois will drive you... where you have to go. But I have a bit of business to attend to, even as you do! And I'll see you when my... business is finished."

The girl smiled up at him, and for all the fripperies of fashion, a feral strength showed in her black eyes, in the slow, cruel movements of her lips. "Business, Martin?" she asked softly. "Business… or murder?"

Martin Wolf's laughter was deep and rumbling. It crowded the tonneau of the car. "As a matter of sober fact," he said softly. "There is no difference tonight. It's murder, but it's important business. I have a date to kill… the Spider!"

The girl's smile wavered a moment on her rich lips. "You speak very glibly," she said. "Will it be as easy as that?"

Martin Wolf nodded, and his solid long lips curved mockingly. "As easy at that," he said crisply. "His friends and allies already are… removed. The bait for the Spider himself has been scattered all over the city tonight—poisoned bait. A reception has been prepared for him at the other aerie. Oh, he'll come, never doubt it. He'll come to snare the Silver Falcon, but he'll find it a dangerous task!" Martin Wolf's nostrils flared and the thick lids drooped a little over his eyes. He laughed again and the girl prettily stopped her ears with her fingers.

"Martin," she whispered. "Martin, when you laugh like that, you… you *terrify* me!"

Martin Wolf stopped laughing and turned the narrow glint of his eyes on her. "Nothing ever terrified you, Vixen," he said softly. "That's why I work with you. But you use your teeth where I tell you… and keep them out of *me!*"

They eyed each other, and there was in both of them the same restrained ferocity, the same cold sureness. Slowly, the two of them smiled into each other's eyes. The girl leaned forward and

• *RICHARD WENTWORTH*

opened a compartment in the back of the front seat, poured out brandy into two racked glasses.

"Your health, Wolf," she said softly, "and death to the Spider!"

Martin Wolf's teeth showed long and pointed, "Your health, Vixen! *And death to the Spider!*"

AT NINETY-SIXTH STREET, the railroad pops out from under Park Avenue and becomes an elevated train—and at that point Park Avenue abruptly changes from a swank residential district to a section of street markets and second-hand furniture shops—to tenement buildings and cold-water flats. The slamming clatter of the speeding trains resounds day and night and the minor noises of living, or dying, are blotted out.

It was into this section that presently, the Spider wheeled his shabby and powerful car to park it amid shadows on a side street. The hooded spectacles of Blinky McQuade had long since been removed and now he took from his mouth the deforming plugs, replaced the gray-shot wig of Blinky McQuade with lank, black hair. Those few changes made a startling alteration in Wentworth's face. It was no longer dissolute, but hawk-beaked, sinister... and predatory! His mouth was a lipless gash and his

eyes shot pale fire from beneath beetling black brows. This was no more the cultured countenance of Richard Wentworth than it was the loose-lipped Blinky McQuade. It was a face from which criminals shrank in terror—the face of the Spider!

From the bundle he carried, Wentworth pulled out a slouch black hat whose broad brim pulled low over his brows. He flung about his shoulders a long cape and, once more, his hand went briefly to the automatic beneath his left arm, which now had been joined by a twin in a holster on the opposite side. Wentworth smiled briefly then, and stepped to the sidewalk. The cold-swept street was deserted, the silhouette of the Spider showed only transiently, then his becaped figure merged with the black shadows of the tenements—and disappeared!

In the shadows of the elevated train tracks was the "other aerie" of the Silver Falcon and the roofs would give the Spider ready access when the time was ripe. But not too soon. Not before the Silver Falcon himself had flown to the nest; not before his plans had been revealed... Across the roofs glided a shadow of hunched shoulders, blending with the darkness where chimney-pots and balustrades laid their black tracery across the tenement tops. The Spider made no more sound than the thing whose name he bore. Once he paused sharply, thinking he heard a signal whistle pipe softly behind him somewhere. He crouched Waiting, listening, but it was not repeated. Presently, he crept on again, but there was a warier light in his eyes.

Across the street, taller tenements raised their heads against the gray of the sky. Behind him, too, were higher buildings. There was only this block of four tenements whose roofs led to the aerie in the one nearest the railroad tracks—a cheap gambling dive that long before *this* had been used as a meeting place of criminals. Once, the Spider froze in a shadow as a train rocketed past, its stream of yellow lights spilling out into the night, its passengers gaily innocent of the life and death struggle impending beneath their very windows.

Once more, it seemed to Wentworth he caught that thin, piping whistle like the silvery signal recalling a falcon from its prey to the wrist of his keeper. Could it be that....

Presently, flat on his stomach, Wentworth wormed his way to a skylight that reflected gay lights from the room beneath. He could see nothing through the translucent glass, but to his ears came the subdued voices of men and, in an abrupt silence, the click of shaken dice. Wentworth shook his head. It wasn't in the main room of the gambling hall that he must look for the Falcon. He crept away and turned toward the rear of the building, where windows in a blank wall looked down on cluttered clothesline and refuse-littered courts. Light came from one window there, though its shade was tight drawn, and once more the rumble of men's voices.

He nodded. This would be the room and that slight silvery gleam at the top of the window—a wire that reached off into darkness—was the final proof. Wentworth's smile was slight, cold. Along such a wire as that must have sailed the phosphorescent falcon whose crash through the glass had heralded the death of Mug Murdock! Surely, the Falcon didn't intend to repeat that trick here?

Wentworth's narrow eyes followed the direction of the wire

and pointed finally to a tenement building across the courts, but lights from the windows of a higher building spilled across it. The roof was empty. For moments longer, the Spider hesitated and then he made his decision. The back of the building on which he crouched was in utter blackness save for that one, shaded window. His figure in the black cape would be undetectable.

Swiftly, Wentworth pulled from a pocket of the cape a coil of light, silk line—no more than pencil thick. He looped it about a chimney base, rigged a seatless bosun's chair in its other end and dropped it over the side. That silken line might seem slight, but it had a tensile strength of more than seven hundred pounds! The police had found remnants of it before and to them it bore a special name. It was the Spider's web!

Wentworth smiled thinly, as he poised on the brink of the gulf and sent his eyes questing over the roofs a final time. The memory of the signals he thought he had heard stayed him for a moment. Then impatiently, he wrapped the light line about his arm and slid over the verge until he could seat himself in the bosun's chair he had rigged at the other end. He had calculated perfectly. By reaching out his foot, he could rest it on the sill of the window behind which he knew the Falcon's men would meet, presently. Meantime, he swung against a blank wall, in shadow, his black cape a perfect camouflage. He waited....

MINUTES DRAGGED past and gradually, amid the mumble of muted voices inside, Wentworth began to distinguish a few of those who spoke. That curt, monotonous speaker was Knife Hogan, and that other man with the frequent, explosive laugh was Chopper Jackson. They had made a quick trip to the "other aerie"!

"It's cinch money," said Jackson, "according to what the Falcon tells me, and I never said 'no' to easy dough. Not me!" He laughed and there was a harsh, edgy quality to it that bespoke his lack of balance—a born killer.

Knife Hogan said, thinly, "He'd better come soon. I don't stall around waiting—not me. I can make my own money."

Wentworth frowned. What was the bait that could bring such outstanding figures at the beck and call of the Falcon? But the Spider was in time. They were not yet a closely knit organization and that killing of the Mug plainly had been intended to overawe them. If he struck tonight and smashed the Falcon, his men would scatter....

Wentworth smiled—and waited. Now and then he twisted his head about to peer toward that opposite roof, but it remained empty. He could not conquer his feeling of uneasiness. Better to wait on the roof, where maneuvering was easy, until... Wentworth checked, with his hands already tightening about the silken rope. The voices within had stopped!

Grimness crept like an ominous shadow across the resolute face of the Spider as that silence lengthened through the moments. Only one thing could stop so flatly the voices of these killers—the entrance of the Falcon himself! Wentworth released his grip upon the rope and his hand, gliding across his chest, suddenly held the blue-steel weight of a gun! His foot reached tentatively for the windowsill, and he waited.

He was not yet ready; he did not yet know enough of the

Falcon's plans. When the man had spoken, the Spider would smash through that window with blazing guns—and a giant organization of crime would be destroyed before it could take root. But not yet, he cautioned himself. Not yet! The silence was broken by a deep, rumbling voice that carried an overtone of laughter. Wentworth knew, without question, that *this* was the voice of the Falcon! His guess was instantly confirmed....

"Greetings, gentlemen," the voice said. "I'll introduce myself at once. I am the Silver Falcon!"

Wentworth's lips flattened against his teeth at the brazen egoism of that voice and its accent of command. The mere sound of it was enough to tell the Spider that he had done well to take this up-springing dictator of crime so seriously. Men like that could utterly dominate the Underworld....

"Yes, yes, I know you're impatient—" the Falcon ran on, pleasantly—"to hear my plans for making us all millionaires. But first there is another little job to attend to! *I am going to kill the Spider!*"

Silent laugher opened the Spider's lipless mouth and the gun in his hand snouted toward the window. Then he heard—unmistakably this time—the thin piping of a silver-toned whistle! In a flash, Wentworth knew that this whole elaborate set-up had been designed as a trap for him! He had swallowed the bait completely and without question! Fast as was the Spider's brain and instantaneous as was the plan that sprang full-fledged into his brain, it was not quick enough. Even as he threw his muscles into the sudden effort of hurling himself through that window with blazing guns, it was too late.

From a window of the tenement behind him, a dazzling beam of light lashed out, to be instantly blended with others from the ground and from overhead—and the window was flung wide to let out the mocking, deep voice of the still invisible Falcon.

"Won't you step into my parlor, Spider?" the Falcon asked gently. "First, of course, you must drop your guns to the gentleman below. Some of my gallant lads are down there with machine guns. There are some across the way and others above you—with machine guns. So you see, Spider, I really must insist that you step into my parlor!"

The mocker remained out of sight. On all sides was the glint of ready guns... and the lights transfixed the dangling Spider on the wall as helplessly as a writhing insect pinned to a specimen board! And the Spider with useless guns in his hands, threw back his head and laughed!

"Certainly," he said. "Certainly, Falcon, I'll be glad to accept your invitation! It seems that I have underestimated you. Careful of these guns below there," he called. "I value them highly!"

The Spider tossed his guns singly toward the earth below and dexterously stepped to the windowsill—and into the Falcon's ring of killers!

CHAPTER 3
EXECUTION!

SOMEHOW, AS he leaped thus into the face of death, the Spider managed to maintain his mocking smile. His eyes swept the room once and came to rest fixedly on the solidly huge figure of the Falcon against the far wall. There was no gun in the Falcon's hands, but everyone of the other six men in the room held a firearm trained on the Spider's body. There was hatred on the faces of those assembled killers and there was fear. The very tension of their whitened gun hands bespoke their dread of this almost legendary nemesis who confronted them, smilingly, with his hands empty at his sides.

Behind that mocking mask, Wentworth's brain was furiously seeking an escape from his dilemma—an escape that would mean also the Falcon's death. The room was larger than he had expected, fully twenty feet deep by twelve broad with the single window and a narrow door its only exits. The size of the room was an additional menace to Wentworth since it precluded any sudden dash for liberty, even if he could brave the guns of a half-dozen men notorious for their accurate and deadly shooting. Plainly, he must employ strategy, but what direction it should take he could not descry. Wentworth fought against a coldness of despair that worked bitterly within him. His spirit alone refused to accept what his coolly calculating mind discerned: tonight, the Spider was doomed!

After that single swift estimate of the situation, Wentworth's eyes centered exclusively upon the person of the Falcon, estimated the hard-boned face with its heavy-lidded intelligent eyes, the knobby protuberance of the forehead. No doubt of the brain power represented there. The mouth was brutally ruthless, despite the almost jovial smile that curved its solid lips now. The size of the man, the shock of fiery hair that rose like a crest from the high brows, caused Wentworth to narrow his eyes in amazement. Give this man the padded fat of Iron Mike and they might be twins for size. In his present guise he more closely resembled a fellow-member of the Adventurers' club whom Wentworth knew only slightly: a big game hunter named Dacey Hunt... Wentworth's estimate of the man and the scene was flashingly made in the few seconds it took him to step lightly over the windowsill and take his stand amid the killers. He nodded jauntily.

"This is pleasant of you, Falcon," he said quietly. "And much more comfortable than my perch outside your window." His eyes went deliberately from face to face about the room. "Knife Hogan," he said. "Chopper Jackson, Milano, Craven, Sako, and the Big Mick. Your company is well chosen, Falcon. All gallows birds together."

The Falcon's big laugh boomed out though the tight hatred of those other killers was intensified. "It's a shame," he said. "It's really a shame to kill you, but you're the last obstacle to my plans and you must be removed."

Wentworth lifted his brows sardonically. "The last? Of course there's the little matter of some nineteen thousand police under a quite able commissioner—my dear friend and enemy, Stanley Kirkpatrick."

The Falcon's smile lingered on his lips. "Stanley Kirkpatrick was stricken with heart disease tonight," he said softly. "At least the doctors will think it is heart disease. He is confined to his bed and within a week, he will be dead!"

"You lie!" Wentworth snapped, then immediately bowed his apology.

But he had betrayed his concern and he saw the exultant gleam in the Falcon's eyes. He realized that the man would have no reason to lie, and that by his outburst he had betrayed his own tension. But good God—how had the Falcon managed to reach Kirkpatrick with poison, as he was hinting! This was genuine disaster! Without Kirkpatrick's strong, intelligent hand at the helm, the police force would be stripped of half its power... Abruptly, Wentworth shut his mind to the torturing knives of his fresh despair. He could have only one thought now—*escape!*

Abruptly, the Falcon tossed him a pack of cigarettes and a book of matches....

"It's time for you to be nonchalant, Spider," he said mockingly. "I have more news for you. I want you to realize fully the utter hopelessness of the situation before I... *remove* you."

WENTWORTH SHRUGGED and lit a cigarette with a hand that was without a tremor. He smiled slightly at that lean, hardened hand of his and an unconscious pang shot through him. Was that dexterous member to become a useless inert thing? Was death... He shook the thought out of his mind as he flicked the match carelessly to the floor.

There had been a time when he had carried many gadgets with him—trick cigarettes that might disorganize an entire room with gas or through which he could discharge a tiny, poisoned dart; but he had found himself growing to depend on these aids, as the killers about him leaned upon their guns. The Spider could not afford to trust his life to such feeble mechanical aids. They could not take from him his brain—except by death! He set himself to receive placidly the new blows which

the Falcon promised. Whether cruelty moti-
vated the man, or whether he wished to
drive Wentworth to despair did not greatly
matter… Wentworth smoked and his keen,
shadowed eyes kept constant watch. The least
wavering of the guards about him, and he
would spring into violent, lethal action. But
there was no wavering….

"I intend—" the Falcon went on softly, and Wentworth
realized that it was all part of a campaign speech to the criminals about him—men not yet sold on the Falcon as a leader—"I intend to loot the city and make us all millionaires by
the application of intelligence to crime. One thing that intelligence dictates, you'll agree, is the removal of every possible
obstacle, such as yourself, *ante facto*… that is to say, before the
fact. Kirkpatrick is out of the way. You…" The Falcon was tick-
ing them off on his fingers. "By this time, that troublesome
fellow, Wentworth—who occasionally steals your thunder—
has been arrested for murder. That surprises you? Oh, it was a
simple matter, I assure you. A mere matter of planting the body
of one of his known enemies in his home and then tipping off
the police!"

Wentworth had barely controlled a start at the man's careless
words. Plainly, as yet, the Falcon did not suspect that the Spider
and Richard Wentworth were the same man. Was it possible that a murdered man's body had been planted there? Then
what of Nita van Sloan… *Nita!* Wentworth was conscious of an

inward tightening of his whole body; a compression about his heart, his very soul. God, let nothing happen to Nita....

"And to show you the thoroughness with which I attend to such things, Spider," the Falcon went on casually, "I even took the trouble to remove Wentworth's woman who at times has proved... difficult."

"For my friend, Wentworth," the Spider said softly, "I will take exception to your phraseology—you mannerless lout!"

The Falcon stiffened, took a half-stride forward before he checked himself. An angry flush burned up his throat, suffused his temples. The effort he made at self-control knotted his huge fists at his sides and despite his anxiety, Wentworth had to slit his own eyes to hide the gleam of exultation that sprang up in them. He had touched a sore spot with this would-be dictator of the Underworld. Perhaps, he could goad him into some rash action that would permit the Spider to close with his foe!

The Falcon's laughter had a forced harsh note. "You have... courage, Spider. But to return to my enumeration. My brave lads and I are planning tomorrow to loot the Metropole Museum of its priceless art objects and so we removed—removed—even Nita van Sloan, as tomorrow we will kill anyone who stands in our way. Nita is now more or less comfortably established in a private madhouse...."

Wentworth now took a slow stride forward this time and drew the tautly held guns like compass needles with him. "So you war on women, too?" he asked, raspingly. "You amateur gentleman! You who hide behind a half-dozen guns to confront me! Surely, you who plan so beautifully have no reason to fear the Spider? Of course not!"

Wentworth's heart was sore within him. He realized that his disbelief of the man's assertions was merely his frantic hope. If the man could have planted the body of a murdered man in his closely guarded home, it would have been simple enough to carry Nita off and to arrange the horror that he described.

Suddenly, Wentworth saw the way in which he might attack this man and perhaps force a situation from which he might hope to escape. The Falcon had an inordinate pride, and he wanted to impress these killers... The Falcon was smiling with a thin, compressed mouth.

"You are about to demand, no doubt," he said softly, "that I meet you in personal combat to prove I do not fear you? I have had, from the first, every intention of obliging you... One of those duels, Spider, for which you are famous. Shall it be with knives, swords or pistols? It is for you to say!"

Wentworth heard the quivering indrawn breath of the men who circled him with ready guns, and their surprise was scarcely less than his own—nor their admiration. It was another flourish to cement their allegiance, of course. Wentworth fought down the hope that flared in his breast. This was ridiculous. The Falcon might go through with the semblance of a duel, but the result would be predetermined—the Spider's death! No matter! Let him once have a chance at moderately free movement! Let these guns relax for an instant... Wentworth forced impassivity upon his face.

"I wouldn't wish to take advantage of you, Falcon," he said

suavely, "but if there happens to be a pair of matched sabers in your armory...."

The Falcon clicked his heels, "Certainly!" His smile widened. "The choice suits me admirably!"

WENTWORTH LOOKED calmly about the room once more—his glance took in the lighting which depended on a single dangling bulb with a reflector. The Falcon had lifted a small silver whistle to his mouth and blew a light double-blast. Instantly, the door at his elbow opened and a man in the somber garb of a valet presented a sword case to the Falcon, and retired—but not before Wentworth had seen two men with drawn guns in the hallway. It added nothing to the difficulty of his situation.

Death ringed him in and, if there was a way out, Wentworth's keen brain still had not found it! He struggled against a feeling of rank incredulity. It was fantastic that not many hours ago, he had been dining sumptuously at his own home, had felt a restlessness that goaded him to seek... adventure! Wentworth almost laughed aloud. God! He had found it, but now Nita, and Kirkpatrick....

Fantastic though this murder-trap might seem, with its promise of bloody imminent death, it was real enough. This giant of a man deftly removing coat and vest across the room might seem like a figure out of the pages of a book, but his sword would bring death no less readily for that! Wentworth felt the taut readiness of his thighs and calves. No, he had small hope of escaping with his life, but if this man spoke truth about Nita and Kirkpatrick, there would be at least a vengeance! And a chance to deliver the people from one last menace before the Spider died! If he must be slain here, the Falcon should die with him!

Wentworth put his eyes wholly on the Falcon. The man seemed even larger without the careful tailoring of his discarded coat. The saber lay like a toy in his immense hand, and Wentworth smiled thinly as the fiery-headed giant made the blade whisper viciously through the air. The Falcon would be proud of his strength and the ceiling was high enough to permit him a full overhead blow in his slashing attack. He might even forget what many sabreurs were prone to overlook—that a saber also has a point! It had been with that thought that Wentworth had deliberately chosen a slashing weapon! It came to his mind fleetingly that the Falcon, sure of his strength and ability, might even fight fairly!

Scarcely had the thought brushed the Spider's consciousness when a faint, quick beam of light thrust on his notice and, under the mask of his bushy, false brows, Wentworth's eyes lifted to a high corner of the room. A bitter smile thinned his lips.

He had been too generous in his estimate of the Falcon! The beam of light had stabbed through a loophole and now, in that miniature aperture of the wall, there glinted the thickened muzzle of a silenced gun!

"You'll forgive me," the Falcon said mockingly, "if I do not offer you the sabers at close range. It might afford you... possibilities. Make your choice now, sir!"

Wentworth had not discarded his cape. He thumbed it back from his arms now so that it bunched between his shoulders, tugged the broad brim of his black hat a little lower over his brows.

"I am sure I can trust so courteous an enemy," he said dryly. "The saber in your right hand will serve."

He was ready.

Scarcely had the words left his mouth when the saber spun through the air toward him. Wentworth caught it neatly and lifted the point, let his experienced eye run along its highlighted blade. Beautiful steel—but deliberately flawed so that it would break in the middle. Wentworth drew a slow breath, let his eyes flick toward the silenced gun at its loophole—and suddenly he flung back his head and laughed. It was not mockery, nor yet bravado. It was the sheer courage of a brave man laughing at Death itself, challenging....

Wentworth flashed the faulty blade up to his chin in salute, then raked out the point on guard, set his left fist lightly on his hip, a gallantly alert figure.

"When you are ready, Falcon," he said softly.

With a booming shout that racketed back from the close wails, the Falcon hurled his great body to the attack!

CHAPTER 4
TO THE DEATH!

EVEN AS the Falcon leaped to the attack, Wentworth had formed his plan of action. The faulty saber in his hand would not stand against a single direct blow of the Falcon's mighty arm, which made parrying a delicate and difficult thing.

34

It meant that the Spider must depend on footwork in a room that already was crowded with men, and under the muzzle of that loop-hole gun!

He laughed as the Falcon sprang lithely forward, incredibly light on his feet for so huge a man, and aimed a blow intended to shatter Wentworth's saber and end the duel instantly with a downward slash into the left side of the throat. He almost achieved his design of ending the fight with that one blow.

Never a conventional swordsman, Wentworth did not make the conventional high parry to that downward slash. Instead, he took the wild chance of knocking aside the saber by a quick side-swung blow of the hilt, and at the same instant he leaped straight forward past the Falcon! It was a desperate chance and one that only the perfectly coördinated muscles and eyes of the Spider could have accomplished. But the saber of the Falcon was deflected just enough and, as he sprang past the Falcon, Wentworth swung the cutting edge of the blade outward in a backhanded slash for the Falcon's unguarded throat!

Death reached out its clawed bony hand for the Falcon in that moment. The drag of that cutting edge could behead a man, and the Spider would press the stroke home without mercy! Instinct must have warned the Falcon. His eyes could not have detected that stroke in time to save him. He bent double and the Spider's saber flashed past so closely over his head that it sheared off a lock of red hair. The Falcon did not check his lunge. He took two gigantic leaps forward before he whirled against the farther wall, his breath short, the sudden sweat glistening

on his forehead. His blade whipped up in a frantic guard… But the Spider was not attacking.

Close against the wall where a moment ago the Falcon had stood, Wentworth confronted his enemy with a quiet smile. By that swift attack, he had reversed their positions—and placed himself where no bullet from that loophole sniper could possi-

He felt the point strike, the weight of the Falcon's bulk

against it—but the saber snapped off clean!

bly reach him! Wentworth reached out with the tip of his sword and flicked the fallen lock of fiery hair into the air.

"I shall have your scalp yet, Falcon," he said mockingly. "What? Are you tired already?"

The Falcon made no answer and, though anger twisted the lines of his solid lips into a snarl, his advance was cautious this time. He glided across the floor with his saber on guard before him, and Wentworth waited for the attack with no more than a yard of space between his shoulders and the wall. He had to stay there. His margin of safety from that hidden gun was narrow at best. Let him so much as lunge and that silenced weapon would drill him in the back—in the same instant that the Falcon would strike over his death-stopped guard to butcher him! Easy enough then for the Falcon to claim that he had bested the Spider in hand-to-hand conflict. His prestige would mount enormously in the Underworld. Wentworth's lips were compressed in a set grim smile....

With a lightning whirl, the Falcon's blade slashed shoulder high, glanced off the Spider's carefully sloping parry and whirled in a violently driven back-cut for the legs. It was a beautifully calculated maneuver and the only sword-parry Wentworth could make would inevitably result in breaking his flawed blade off short! Instead, Wentworth sprang lightly into the air and cut for the Falcon's face! The Falcon leaped backward out of reach, and once more the Spider did not follow his advantage.

The Falcon sneered at him, a brutal distortion of the heavy face. "Surely, Spider, you are not afraid of a bit of steel? Come

out of your corner, little one. I will not hurt you too much…
too long!"

WENTWORTH MADE no answer except for his set
smile. His eyes clung to the gaze of the Falcon, but he was not
unaware of the six killers pressed close against the walls of the
room. They still held their guns, but they did not now swivel
with the Spider's every movement. Their faces were intent. Knife
Hogan touched his tongue to dry lips. He had always had a
mania for work with cold steel, and there was lust in his eyes—
the lust to see that keen bright steel buried in a man's vitals! Not
quite so alert, but they were still ready with their guns, and even
if he succeeded in felling the Falcon….

Wentworth shook the thought out of his mind. At least, he
could see all his enemies now, except for the hidden gunner
behind the loophole!

His attention swung rigidly back to the Falcon, and it was
time! With no warning at all except the slight tightening of the
eyes that Wentworth had spotted, the Falcon leaped forward
in a slashing attack that took all the Spider's practiced skill to
turn. The Falcon had given up hoping for an easy victory and his
assault had a three-fold purpose: to break the Spider's sword, to
drive him to a spot where the silenced gun could drill him or to
kill him with his slashing, razor-keen saber!

The musical note of the steel filled the room, the heavy stamp
of the Falcon's feet. Wentworth stood almost motionless save
for the sway of his shoulders, the swift play of his sword arm.
Time and again, it seemed impossible for him to ward a slash
without taking a direct blow that would shatter the sword, but

he contrived. It was doubly difficult since he wished the Falcon to
concentrate all his attention on the
edge and forget the thrusting point
of the saber. It would have been much
easier, could Wentworth have poised
the blade rapier-like before him and
kept the point darting at the Falcon's eyes.

Wentworth fought almost wholly on the defensive, biding
his chance. The Falcon's breath gusted out with the violence of
his strokes. Never had the Spider opposed a man who combined
such strength with lightning speed. It was a stupendous feat, but
Wentworth did not believe that even the Falcon could keep it
up indefinitely. Yet, only in extremity would the Falcon call on
the men around him for help. He would lose face and this whole
battle had been intended to build him up in the eyes of these
killers. It was for this reason, Wentworth continued barely to
evade the sword. He even slowed the movements of his blade
so that it seemed he succeeded only by a hair's breadth in saving
himself, time and again. It was a perilous, a mad thing to do
against such a swordsman as the Falcon, but it was the only
way. And once more the Spider had a plan, a scheme that would
begin with the death of the Falcon....

Wentworth made an abortive, awkward cut at the Falcon's
right shoulder and it was brushed aside. In return, the Falcon's
saber swished at the Spider's head. He avoided it by a swift
dodge and his hat was swept from his head. The Falcon laughed
and pressed his advantage. The saber made a constant circle of

light. Wentworth had lost his smile. His teeth were bared by shrinking lips in seeming desperation and his breath hissed in distended nostrils. He swayed a little, his feet shuffled as he fumbled aside.

"You are finished, Spider," the Falcon boomed. "In another moment, you'll feel my edge in your throat. Your head shall become a football for the Underworld!"

As he spoke, he leaped close and whipped his saber down in another such severing slash as he had launched at the beginning of the duel. For an instant, Wentworth opposed his own blade in a high parry, and he saw exultation leap into the Falcon's eyes, saw his muscles tauten as he prepared to drive that stroke home. For it was the kind of parry the Spider had been avoiding throughout the battle—the kind that would snap his sword off short! And Wentworth put fear into his own widening eyes.

Once more, Wentworth called on his splendid sense of timing, his carefully tutored body for a desperate and lightning-fast maneuver. The sword which had been poised on guard whipped about so that its point was toward the Falcon's breast. No time to bring that arm down and drive home.

Even as Wentworth's wrist brought the point about, he was hurling himself almost head-first forward under the Falcon's sword arm!

No swordsman could have turned that blow aside. The Falcon could not check the downswing of his saber and a broken shout tore from his lips. Triumph was warm in the Spider's throat though he knew that an instant after his blade plunged home,

41

his back would be exposed to the loophole sniper behind the wall. He had planned for that, too.

He felt the point strike, felt the weight of the Falcon's bulk against it. But instead of driving into flesh, Wentworth felt a numbing shock against his sword hand as if from a punch. The saber bowed, snapped off clean!

Wentworth did not see these things since he was bent double, dodging forward, but he felt the wrench and heard the singing metallic note as the steel broke. A harsh curse tore from his throat! No need to guess what had happened. Under his clothing, the Falcon wore chain mail!

Anger burned through the Spider's heart—and carried despair with it. All his advantage of position and surprise was gone, his sword broken, his back exposed to the sniper. Even in the midst of defeat, the Spider swept boldly into action. A second stride carried him beyond the Falcon and his broken sword swept up over his head and slashed at the electric wires of the single dangling light! The contact was made in a flash of blue light and a jarring shock ran along Wentworth's sword hand, numbed his entire arm—*but the light went out!*

IN THE darkness, Wentworth flung the flat and mocking laughter of the Spider's at his enemies. He checked his stride even as he was striking at the electric wires and, with the stroke, pivoted again toward the Falcon! He had recognized the danger of that shock and his left hand whipped across, caught the broken sword before it could drop from his paralyzed grip. On the retinas of his eyes, the figure of the Falcon was still plain. He had been reeling, off balance, a hand braced against the wall, his

42

sword arm almost limp. The point of Wentworth's sword, despite the mail, had deliv-
ered now an almost paralyzing heart punch.

It was not in fury that the Spider struck
this final time, but in a cold and calm judg-
ment of justice. The man had boasted of
intended slaughter and looting, had gathered killers about him. It was mete that he
should be executed before he could carry

out his fearful plans... The Spider struck with his broken sword,
and hit only the wall! Violently, he flung himself to the right.
The shouts of men were dinning in his ears. A gun sent its crimson gash of flame across the darkness of the room and a scream
answered it—a scream of anguish. Wentworth stumbled against
a tall and heavy man whose hands closed with fierce power,
instantly, on Wentworth's throat!

Wentworth's left hand, with all the weight of his surge behind
it—with all the drive of his shoulder and powerful back—
reached up and thrust... above the body that mail could protect!
A scream answered and the hands whipped from his throat. The
scream was strangled, bubbling, awful... Wentworth reeled back,
dropped instantly to his knees. He heard a liquid spattering on
the floor, but no body thumped to the floor. Cautiously, Wentworth stretched out a hand, felt the spasmodically jerking legs
of the man he had killed—had just nailed to the wall with his
broken sword!

Death stumbled past within a few inches of where the Spider
crouched and once more a gun blasted. Instantly, three other

guns answered it. And the Spider smiled grimly in the darkness; If they wanted to shoot at each other, he would give them a target. With a crisp movement, he swept off the cape and flung it about the stilled body of the man he had slain. Then he crept toward the door.

It would be easy, with his deft skill, to slaughter these killers as they richly deserved, but they were terrified men now without a leader. It would be long before they recovered from their fear of the Spider sufficiently to enter again upon the lists of crime. Beside the door, Wentworth paused and slipped a cigarette lighter from his pocket. His heart was beating high with hope. If the Falcon had told the truth about Nita and Kirkpatrick, a way could be found now to circumvent that. The frame-up of murder against himself... Wentworth shook his head. It could be solved now that the Falcon was dead!

Wentworth's lips were smiling as he pressed the base of his cigarette lighter to the wall. When the lights came on again, the killers who were left alive would find the vaunting signature of the Spider upon his work, a sprawling figure, sinister with its hairy legs and poison fangs—*the seal of the Spider!*

Wentworth's hand closed on the door knob. He turned it slowly. There had been gunners out here, but they were in the dark now, for the slashing of the electric cord had short-circuited the fuses. He would fling wide the door and let them empty their weapons into their companions. When the fight was over... Wentworth whipped open the door and violent white light slashed into his face! It was then that he heard, raspingly loud in the room, the voice of the Falcon!

"There by the door! Burn him down, men! Burn down the Spider!"

While the Falcon's words still rang out, the Spider was in desperate motion. Chagrin warped his features. He had been sure the Falcon was dead, and now there was no chance to make certain of that. There would be no more grace period, no more travesty of a duel. If they caught the Spider this time, it would be after his body had been pumped full of lead! This was no time for bravado, or mad defiance. The Spider must flee for his life!

The same marvelous coordination that had enabled him to defeat the Falcon in the duel stood him in good stead. He had not waited for the Falcon's words to act, but on the instant the white light struck him, he was attacking! Headlong, from his crouch beside the door, he had dived straight for the blazing flashlight that blinded him! He heard guns speak out, felt the concussion of the shots, but they were aimed by suddenly terrified men—by criminals used to shooting their victims in the back and now confronted, face-to-face, by the nemesis they feared more than all the forces of the law!

Their first shots raked wildly above his head and cursing rage burst out in the room. There were screams of pain, too, and furious men fired at each other blindly in the darkness. They were bound by no ties of loyalty, and killing was their trade. They... killed, but their target was not the Spider. It was the gun-flashes of their allies!

Wentworth's long leap swept the flashlight from a man's hand and crashed it into darkness. His out-reaching arms clamped around the assassin and the drive of his tackle hurled them both to the floor. The gunman's head slammed against the wall and his muscles jerked and went limp. Wentworth caught the man's gun from his relaxing hand, made a single long silent leap forward into the darkness and crouched motionless. Guns blazed down at the figure on the floor—a storm of lead screamed through the hall.

Prone on the floor, Wentworth wormed his way to a doorway and squeezed himself into its protection. Then he waited. Somewhere down that hall, the Falcon still lurked. When he came out of hiding, when this mad gun-battle of terror was finished, he would find the Spider ready for him!

Wentworth knew well the risk he ran in remaining on this spot. It was only a question of time before the Falcon would succeed in organizing these men, and start a quest for the Spider. Moreover, the gun battle would bring scores of police to the scene. A few shots might have escaped attention under the shadow of the railway, but *this* fusillade would alarm the entire neighborhood... And it would be equally fatal to the Spider, if he should fall into the hands of the police! Some few of them might recognize that the Spider fought on their side, but they could not ignore the fact that his red seal had been printed on the forehead of many a slain man. That those men richly deserved death; that their demise served the ends of justice could not change the verdict of the law—it was murder. And yet... the Spider waited!

FRANTIC CALLS echoed through the hallway now, but not from the men who had been set in ambush there. The attack of the Spider, and stream of lead from the doorway, had wiped them out. The guns were suddenly still and, after their thunder, the silence was an aching, tangible thing. Not even a voice sounded. Through the quiet, there came the distant swift rumble of a train, the first faint whisper of a siren. Then abruptly, panic feet beat out their stuttering rhythm of flight, but it was on the floor beneath Wentworth!

A curse burst from his locked teeth, and instantly his keen mind flew to the solution. That loophole sniper should have told him before this that there was a passage between the walls. Now it was clear that there was a stairway there to the floor below. Wentworth sprang up and on silent feet raced toward the steps in the hallway, but the retreat was far ahead of him. He sprinted on to a window that gave on the street, crouched behind the glass to watch for the Falcon. It was useless. He knew that though his heart prompted him to hope. Not by any such public means would the Falcon take flight.

Still the Spider crouched there through long seconds while the sirens whooped nearer and the street emptied of fugitive rats. Finally, he thrust to his feet. The numbness had long since gone from his right arm, but he knew a sudden access of fatigue. The tension of those long minutes, the life and death struggle, were taking their toll. He straightened his shoulders, shook off his weariness as he hurried along the death-strewn hallway. He stumbled a little....

A POLICE radio car slammed into the street before the hidden gambling hall, within thirty seconds, and others rocketed to the scene on its heels, but it was fully two minutes before they established a cordon around the bullet-blasted hideout of the Falcon. Before that time, Wentworth had worked his way across the roofs and, shaken by his exertions, managed to escape the law's net.

He was forced to abandon his car which was within the police lines. He was hatless, without an overcoat in the biting cold of the midnight hours—a conspicuous figure should the widening circle of police spot him. His defeat by the Falcon—for he counted it that—rankled deeply, and with it the knowledge that he had failed to disrupt the Falcon's organization before it could form. He had not even prevented the effort to impress the gang of newly assembled killers, if the Falcon had actually succeeded in displacing Kirkpatrick and in framing a murder plot against Wentworth himself!

Wentworth stopped near a corner luncheon stand place to still his panting breath, then pushed rapidly inside and sought out the phone booth that stood at its rear.

It was typical of the man, Wentworth, that his first call was not to his own home about the frame-up or even to ascertain the safety of the woman he loved, Nita van Sloan, but to the office of the commissioner of police, Stanley Kirkpatrick! For the forces of the law must be informed of this new menace! No matter what crimes might seem to have been committed in Wentworth's own home, Kirkpatrick would at least listen to the warning. Their friendship would not deter the commissioner from tracking Wentworth down, but he would take intelligent action against the Falcon... if the Falcon had not already "removed" him!

Wentworth's hand tightened painfully about the telephone

receiver while he waited for his call to go through. He found himself holding his breath....

"Commissioner Kirkpatrick," he snapped when police head-quarters answered. "Richard Wentworth calling."

"Commissioner Kirkpatrick is temporarily away," the man reported automatically. "I can connect you with the secretary of the acting commissioner, Mr. Hunt."

"Who?" Wentworth demanded incredulously.

"Mr. Dacey Hunt, sir."

Wentworth groped the receiver for the hook. The Falcon was fulfilling his boast, but... *Dacey Hunt!* Good God, was it possible that his guess concerning the Falcon's possible identity was so soon confirmed? Dacey Hunt was the name of the fellow member of the Adventurers' Club whom Wentworth knew slightly, a gigantic, fiery-headed man like the Falcon himself!

Well, the Spider would investigate that similarity—and the strange appointment of Dacey Hunt to Kirkpatrick's post so soon after he had been stricken! He must get through some-how to Kirkpatrick's side and warn him. It would be worse than useless to give his information to the police. Even if they believed him—and there had been no charges against him—they would scarcely know how to move against a criminal of the Falcon's type. Wentworth tried to force these deliberate cold thoughts through his mind, but a riot of fear was within him. If the Falcon could so easily strike down the commissioner of police, what hope was there for Nita! Wentworth's mouth was drawn knife-thin. He waited tautly while a distant buzzing came over the wires. Again, again....

The click of a lifting receiver drew every muscle in his body tense, but the first syllables of the man's voice that answered told him that… that Nita was gone, though that voice only said gravely, "Wentworth's residence." For he knew at once that it was a voice he had never heard before, and it meant that the police were in charge of his residence and were maintaining their usual practice of answering all phone calls that came into suspected quarters. Wentworth felt dark despair writhe through his heart, but he forced himself to hope.

"I'd like to speak to Miss van Sloan," he said, and tried to keep the eagerness of his faint hope from his voice.

"I'm sorry," the policeman answered. "Miss van Sloan is not here. Who's calling, please? If I could take a message…" The man's voice ran on conventionally, but very slowly, very deliberately.

Bitterness twisted Wentworth's mouth. The old trick! Trying to hold him while the call was traced, while radio cars were sent racing across the city to seize him. He needed no farther confirmation of the Falcon's threat against himself! He had been framed for murder all right. With anger biting at his soul, Wentworth flung from the booth and fled as rapidly as he could without attracting attention. Already, he could catch the harping of a siren in the distance.

It was not enough that Kirkpatrick had been torn from control of the police and that Nita had been taken. He, himself, must flee like a hounded rabbit. Every uniformed man he passed became a point of danger, yet somehow he must crash through that peril and reach Kirkpatrick's side, to warn and save him. He must find some new way to track down and slay the Falcon. He knew where to hunt at least! On his breast, the Falcon would wear the bruise that his saber-point had made through the mail the man had worn!

Running lightly through the dark byways, streaking toward his new objective, the Spider threw back his head and laughed. It was a flat and mocking sound, a sinister thing to hear in the blackness of the night. If Dacey Hunt had such an injury, a bruise above his heart—*the Spider would strike!*

CHAPTER 5
WHERE THE FALCON FLIES

I N T H E office of the commissioner of police, Dacey Hunt stood with his fiery red head thrown up challengingly and his huge fists knotted together behind him. There was a scowl on his face as he confronted the sergeant and the girl just inside the doorway. The girl was exquisite in a dark, bold way. Her gown, of drooping silk, molded the litheness of hips and thighs between the richness of her thrown-back furs. It seemed to be at her that Hunt was scowling but there was an appreciative gleam in his narrow eyes and something suspiciously like a smile lurked in the corners of his solid lips.

"So," he said softly, "you wish to make a complaint against Richard Wentworth? What is the nature of this complaint and who are you?"

The girl took a quick step forward so that the sergeant could no longer see her face and the lid of her right eye fluttered in

the faintest of winks. Afterward, her challenging eyes dropped modestly.

"I am Moire Shovic," she said hesitantly. "I'm Lou Lydon's... friend. He went tonight to the house of this man, Wentworth, to collect a gambling debt. Oh, I warned him against it, but he

In that charnel madness
a few men were already
looting the ticket booths!

only laughed at me. He did say that if he wasn't back in a couple of hours, I should tell some… some of the boys. I thought it was better to come to you, because—*he hasn't come back!*"

Dacey Hunt threw back his head in booming laughter that seemed to make the walls vibrate, and he thumped a fist solidly into a thick palm. "By God, Sergeant," he cried, "this cinches the case against Wentworth! Now we have the last thing we needed—a motive for the kill! Call in stenographers to take *this* girl's statement. There is no need to check on her identity. I have seen her in Lou Lydon's before this…."

The sergeant saluted, though there was a slightly puzzled frown on his forehead, and left the office to give the order. Moire Shovic strolled forward and hitched herself up to a seat on the commissioner's desk, sat there swinging her silken ankles.

"I'm glad I can supply what you want," she said softly.

Dacey Hunt's laughter boomed out again and he leaned closer. "Vixen," he said, "you're priceless. When this business in finished, we'll see if you can… supply what *I* want!"

The Vixen's eyes remained completely demure, fixed on her swinging ankles. "You're a queer bird for a police commissioner," she said. "A very queer bird…."

They were like that when the jangling of the emergency bell from the police news ticker in a corner of the room brought the sergeant back into the office at a dead run. He stared down at the paper jerking across the clattering machine and then he spun with a white, worried face toward the huge acting commissioner of police.

"It's murder, sir!" he gasped. "Murder and a riot in the Grand Central Terminal!"

GRAND CENTRAL terminal, as always on the night before a holiday weekend, was a noisy, bustling place. The concourse bore its burden of thousands of human beings, pouring in casual, winding rivers toward train gates; waiting for friends or loved ones in clusters about the central, clock-crowned information booth, all of them smiling, gay... holiday-bound. Even the over-burdened redcaps seemed to have caught the infectious spirit.

The long queues at the ticket windows uttered no complaint, but laughed and joked among themselves... and poured thousands of dollars into the tills. But no special precautions were being taken against bandits. The railway considered itself pretty safe against ordinary robbers. Of such extraordinary criminals as the Falcon, the railway had no knowledge at all....

Oh, there were railway police in plain-clothes on duty among the crowds, but their chief job was to watch for pickpockets— and the Falcon did not choose his followers from among their petty ranks. There were uniformed men, too, but they were thinking of getting home for their own holidays and their eyes gazed unseeingly on the featureless crowd that poured past them.

There was a particularly big eddy in the flowing rivers of people over at the snow train gate. It wasn't opened yet and men and girls stood in jostling, singing groups, their skis towering over their heads. There was one couple apart and the golden-haired girl, standing close to her lover, was perhaps more observant than the police. She looked toward two men who stood motionless on the outskirts of that crowd and shuddered a little to find their sardonic eyes upon her.

"Really, John—" she turned to the boy beside her—"I don't know whether we want to take this trip or not. Some of the people look so... so sinister!"

John laughed and his arm tightened about her slim waist. "Don't worry, Claire," he whispered. "I can take care of you!" He glowered about him, feeling strong, ready to defy death itself for Claire, and plenty able to do it too! That was what he thought... *then*.

But Claire seemed alone in her apprehensions. Over by the central information booth, a mother kept her two children close to her while her watching eyes ranged across the floor and a worried, half-eager smile touched her lips. But there was no alarm, no fear on her face....

"Mommie!" Her boy turned his face up to her. "Mommie, we'll miss the train if Daddy doesn't come soon, won't we, Mommie? We'll miss the train, won't we, Mommie?"

For an instant the mother turned her eyes to the boy and her eyes softened before she turned back to her watch. "*Sh!* Daddy will be here in plenty of time. Oh, look! There he is now. See him on the steps! Now everything will be all right—won't it dear?"

The boy said, "Yes, Mommie, I guess so... I don't see Daddy. Oh, look, Mommie, what are those men up there doing?" He stared up toward the balcony over the steps where a man peered down at the concourse with a jeering smile on his mouth. Behind him, men were moving big containers like cages. But the boy, who couldn't guess the nature of those men, seemed to be the only one who noticed.

"There's Daddy," his mother insisted. "See him waving a paper! There, go meet him!"

She smiled proudly, drawing her smaller daughter close to her while the boy's bright blue beret wove through the crowd toward his father. Even above the mumble of laughter and many voices, of shuffling feet, she could hear his thin, piping voice calling, "Daddy!"

"I'll stay right here until you get back!" she called after him. She meant it, of course. Why should she think it would be long and long before he came back. It is only the dead who never come back....

Their eager voices reached the ears of a silvery-haired man who stood by the gates of a northbound express and he turned to his diminutive wife beside him, smiling, nodding benevolently. Echoes of their own youth were all about them, in the piping voices of that boy, in the golden-haired girl in the soft blue ski suit and the youth who stood over her so protectively. The hand of the elderly man's wife lifted to his sleeve. No need for these *two* to speak; each knew the other's thoughts too clearly.

She was thinking of fifty years together and the shadow of the smile in his eyes recorded that same memory. Tomorrow it would be fifty years since they had been like that golden-haired girl and the boy with his arm about her—since they had married. They had laughed together and talked of their golden anniversary to come, not really believing such a long-off thing could happen. And now it was tomorrow. Faltering words formed in her old lady's heart, of thanksgiving and prayer. "I thank thee, oh Lord, for these full years together. So many years. There can't be many more, but it has been enough. It has been enough." Her hand clung a little more tightly to her husband's arm. "Not many more, but when it comes, if it be thy will, oh Lord, call us to thy arms *together....*"

The crowd surged and laughed, emptied toward the trains and was constantly renewed; happy, holiday crowds. A prayer on an aged woman's lips, and a boy's shrill voice as he ran toward his father's waiting arms, a golden-haired girl's love-comforted fears... They were like that when all the myriad lights of Grand Central blinked out. Everyone of all those thousands of lights... *out.*

It was incredible and the suddenness of it dropped like a leaden blanket. Feet ceased to shuffle and voices cut off, and a girl's single, light laugh fell belatedly on the gathering silence. It gripped the crowd, that silence. For three, four, five seconds, it was as absolute as death itself except for the distant rumble of a train and a piping air whistle.

It was into that dead silence that the woman *screamed!*

WHO SHALL know what frightened her? Was it the faint, swift whisper of something that hurtled through the air close by? Was it the muffled, sodden sound of a blow in the dark? She screamed... and tore the silence to shreds. A man started to laugh and the mirth was cut short on his lips. A woman who stood close to him felt something warm and wet fly against her face, heard a blow and afterward a hard, scratching sound on the floor at her feet. A hand brushed her ankle but it was without feeling, without grip in the fingers. It was beating, convulsively at the floor.

It was still soon, but the woman didn't know that. Her scream was flung into the mounting bedlam and she turned and fled. She collided against other people and struck out with mad hands; she screamed and ran on and collided and fell and rose and stumbled....

All over that black and crowded hall, men and women were gripped with panic-fear. There was nothing wrong. There could be nothing seriously wrong. But here and there in the darkness, men's and women's voices cut short with that sodden, crunching sound of a blow and afterward they scrabbled, dying, on the floor. A mutter of wild terror ran over those thousands, and became a roar, formless and abject with fear, that poured inchoate from human animals' throats. It was like animals, too, that they stampeded!

A loudspeaker was booming suddenly as some official tried to bring order, but even his magnified voice was beaten down by the mob roar. Here and there a rare flashlight threw its white blade for instants across the darkness. They brushed across tortured faces, tossing arms, across a maelstrom of fighting men and maddened women. Wide-open faces, screaming. Weaker people were falling. By a train gate, an elderly, silver-haired man sheltered a diminutive woman in his arms, but his strength was long since spent. For a while, they were buffeted in that torrent of terror. The man's hat fell and his silvery hair was a pitiful target... for a while. It disappeared.

From that incredible, stunning body of voices, little sounds were tossed up, pitiful tokens of suffering: a woman's wailing call, "Junior! *Junior!*" Twice repeated and crushed down by the tidal roar of terror. A child's shrill scream, sliced off in its midst, a man frantically calling a woman's name. Then brutal, cursing in mechanic rage, the death stammer of a machine-gun! It made a splurge of crimson light for a few instants, flickered on a falling windrow of human bodies—and went out. It was just afterward that a single, rising harsh cry made itself heard, the fierce scream of a hawk!

In that charnel madness, a few men moved with direct purpose. They had been stationed at strategic points, near the ticket offices, and each carried in his hand a gun and a lead-weighted club. Those guns spoke at need, but usually their voices were muted by human flesh close against the muzzles. The men did not have to move far, just to the doors of the ticket offices. They were already coming out again, laden with loot, when the machine-gun spoke for the first time, when the hawk screamed... At intervals, after that, the machine-guns hammered out again, but always farther from the insanity and death of the concourse, carving a path through human walls....

In the streets outside was darkness also, pierced only by the unaccustomed brilliance of scores of automobile headlights. Here, too, death was striking. Not death beneath the panic feet of crowds, but sudden mysterious death that struck from no man knew where and left shattered things to scramble out their lives on the pavement—things that had been men but now were quivering, dying flesh whose skulls were crushed in. A squad car of police battered its way through the traffic chaos and men in blue poured from it, raced toward the vomiting doorways of the Grand Central terminal.

There, too, the death struck. A sergeant, gripping a machine-gun, his mouth grimly set, his eyes narrowed and frantic as he drove forward in a sprint, checked suddenly and stared upward into the night sky. He jerked up the machine-gun... and a shadow struck his face, a shadow that struck with a sound of a sledge-hammer hitting bone.

The sergeant was hurled his length backward to the pavement and did not stir again. His face had *vanished*... Another officer stooped over him, his face twisted, blood-red in incredulity and horror. Once more the shadow passed... There were two men in blue down, two more. The shadows were everywhere, and the sound of sledgehammers swinging and striking, always striking....

FIFTY BLOCKS north on Park Avenue, a man was running, panting through side streets, when far away to the south he saw the city lights black out. It was a sudden slice taken out of the night glow against the black sky, a shadow as ominous as death itself falling across the city. That man was hatless and without a coat. He reeled a little as he ran, but his jaw had a strong, tense line and his head was high. For a moment, when that shadow fell, he stopped and stood utterly motionless, while coldness ran through him and the fearful premonition of disaster. He swerved and darted toward Park Avenue, flung himself to the running-board of a taxi.

"South!" he rasped. "South, and damn the traffic lights!"

The driver twisted about, a sly grin on his mouth. "Yeah?" he

mumbled. "Yeah, and you're the commissioner, I guess—*ain't...*"
His voice died out and his eyes popped wide. "Yes, sir. South—
and damn the lights!"

His fare flung himself back on the seat, closed his eyes and
forced relaxation upon his body. Slowly, his muscles loosened
so that he rolled and jounced limply with the jerks of the cab.
He lifted a gaunt arm to the radio and adjusted it swiftly so that
presently the whine of the police announcer's call came in above
the roar of the racing engine.

"Calling all cars, Grand Central district!" the voice raced.
"Make all possible speed to Grand Central Terminal. Signal
thirty. Signal X!"

The fare's eyes opened and they were gray-blue and burning
under bushy brows. The announcer's voice was racing on, order-
ing out emergency crews and reserves from precinct stations.
"Signal thirty! Signal X!" Murder and riot, those cryptic words
meant. To the man they meant another, more awful thing. They
meant... *the Falcon!*

Yet Richard Wentworth remained almost supine upon the
rear seat. The taxi driver did not now need the goad of his
compelling eyes, of the sinister face of the Spider to drive him on
at top speed. And the Spider must gather his strength for battle.
His hand moved to the holster beneath his arm and he brought
out the one captured revolver he possessed. Three cartridges, and
his own supply would not fit it. His lips twisted bitterly.

He had vauntingly, a few hours before, planned to nip this
colossal conspiracy in the bud; to stop the Falcon before he could
launch his jihad of crime slaughter. He had been mad, mad, and

he himself had been beaten before the start. The entire city had been beaten, conquered. No man remained who could cope with such horror, save only the Spider himself, and he was a fugitive, stripped of allies and friends; robbed even of the facilities, the sinews of such warfare. But the Spider would fight! God yes, he would fight, while he lived....

CHAPTER 6
TWO RED-HEADED MEN

WHEN THE incredible sound of the horror in Grand Central began to hammer at Wentworth's senses, it whipped him tautly forward on his seat, dragged a ragged curse from his lips. There was pain and terror in that overwhelming outcry and there was death. Such mad panic must have poured from the souls of those who fled helplessly from a lava-flooded Pompeii; from San Francisco when quake and fire cracked open the very earth itself! The taxi driver had stiffened at the first taint of that sound upon the air, and suddenly he slammed on brakes and sat with the tremors shaking his cringing shoulders. The street sign on the corner read: 52 *ST E.*

"Hurry, damn you!" Wentworth rasped.

"Not me!" the man quavered. "Not me. I can get killed right here, but I ain't going no farther. I..." He hopped out of the car and began to run. He had traveled no more than thirty feet when a despairing cry burst from his lips.

Wentworth, already climbing in behind the wheel, jerked his head that way. He could see only the faint blur of the running man, his upturned face white with terror, then a darker shadow that swept downward from the night and the sound of a blow. After that, silence....

Wentworth's lips went cold with pressure, but there was nothing he could do for a dead man! He threw the cab in gear and its motor began to hum, to roar. The Spider leaned far forward over the wheel, teeth clamped, hands white with gripping, every sense desperately bent on reaching the scene ahead where the Falcon slew his scores and hundreds. Already Wentworth's keen mind was canvassing the horror that he knew awaited him, seeking the best means of attack. That mounting mingled roar of terror seemed to daze him as it increased, moment by moment, block by block. Curses were driven in a steady stream from his lips. God in heaven! Human beings made that sound! Human beings who were, to the Falcon, only offerings upon the altar of his greed!

A block ahead the traffic was wedged from curb to curb, impassable, and four blocks beyond that were the entrances to the ramp causeways that twisted about the Grand Central Terminal itself and debouched finally onto Park Avenue at Fortieth Street. If he could once gain those... As quickly as the thought struck Wentworth's mind, he acted. He trod the accelerator into the floorboards and wrenched the wheel of the taxi. With a crash, he struck the iron fence that guarded the central parkway which, a narrow strip of grass in the midst of wide sheets of asphalt, separated the two lanes of traffic along Park Avenue.

The taxi faltered, the fence slammed to earth and the Spider roared on to the attack. After that, at each corner, most of the fences were already down, apparently hammered flat by escaping cars. The front tires burst and the windshield blew back in stabbing fragments from its frame. Wentworth did not check and now he gripped in his right fist his captured pistol with its lone three cartridges. His shoulders surged with the effort to guide the cab one-handed, but he did not falter in his forward drive. His lips creased back from his teeth in a savage smile. The Falcon was slaughtering the helpless, and the innocent—but some of the guilty should pay the penalty!

Intent as Wentworth's whole being was on the battle ahead, there was a part of his brain that puzzled over these jammed cars. They were abandoned, most of them. But why? Why hadn't their owners wrenched them about and fled from such horror as they must know lay ahead? And then Wentworth saw the reason! A solid block of reasons. In those motionless cars, many of them jammed in minor wreckage together, there were drivers, but now slumped across the wheels... *dead!* And the windshields bore the starred and sinister scars of bullets!

WENTWORTH'S FURY was a cold and raging thing, but his mind was clicking with the perfection of a nicely adjusted machine. He made his brief survey of those cars, of the patterns of bullet holes and knew that a machine-gun had blasted them from the dark recesses of the ramp which was his own goal! It would still be there, unless the killers already had finished their fearful carnage, and fled. It would be there... The last flattened fence swept under the charge of the taxi. Wentworth wrenched it through an opening between cars, pointed its hood for the ramp—and flung himself to the floor!

With one hand only, he controlled the wheel while he crouched below the level of the taxi's heavy motor. It would guard him against the machine-gun bullets until he could get near enough to see his targets! He felt the vibration of the hurricane of lead, first of all, then the wall-magnified racketing of the machine-gun. The vault of the tunnel through which the ramp rose hurled back the tremendous roar of his engine, the sharp clatter of the gun even above the muted immensity of that other, more sinister roar—the voices of the Falcon's sacrifices, the slaughter-ridden crowd within the station.

Wentworth braced himself rigidly on the floor as the taxi took the upward surge of the ramp. Directly ahead, there was a low concrete abutment and that was where the machine-gunner crouched to pour out death. Wentworth set his feet against the taxi door, toed the catch loose and, gauging his distance carefully, wrenched the cab to the right just as it towered over the low concrete wall. He raised his head and the gun was ready in his hand. His eyes stabbed through the shadows and there was twisted, ugly laughter on his lips.

As he had figured, the machine-gunner was terrified at the unchecked charge of the taxi. He feared that the cab might leap the wall and grind him to bits—and he had sprung to his feet to flee from the path of a monster his bullets could not stop. For a flashing instant, Wentworth had a clear target and in that brief gasp of time, he flung two bullets out through the open doorway. The next instant, the taxi slammed at an angle into the guard wall, reared up and swung violently to the right, its steering-gear finally smashed. The wrench completed what Wentworth already had begun, flung him, feet-first, out through the door he had opened! He hit, rolling, on his hip and shoulder, surged to his feet while his eyes flew to the Falcon's killer.

At least one of the Spider's hastily flung bullets had scored. The man was braced against the back wall of his narrow stronghold, and the machine-gun... Even as Wentworth spotted him, while the momentum of the fall still made him reel on his feet, the man got the machine-gun up and squeezed the trigger. He should have waited an instant longer and made sure of his target. The lead shredded the air within a foot of Wentworth's head, and his pistol spoke once more, speeding his last bullet.

At the same moment, Wentworth hurled himself violently to the attack. He whipped his gun back to throw it, a final desperate gamble with death—but there was no need. At his shot, the machine-gunner had stiffened against the concrete. He held that stance for heartbeats while Wentworth took two long strides and sprang into a high hurdle over the wall. As the Spider's hand closed on his throat and the pistol sang through the air toward the man's head, he went limp.

Wentworth scooped up the machine-gun, slung two extra drums of ammunition over his shoulder by their carrying belt. On the brink of charging on to the battle, he paused. The dead gunner wore a curious kind of helmet. Wentworth had proved it was no proof against bullets, but it strangely resembled the crash helmets which race-car drivers and testers wear, and it was tinted a bright red which seemed madness. Memory came whitely to Wentworth—the memory of a sweeping shadow and a taxi driver who moved no more; and of the Mug who had fallen with a crushed skull in the bit house of Iron Mike. With a quick movement, he freed the red helmet from the dead man and dragged it on over his own head and, with a twisted smile on his lips, he bent to press his seal upon the man's forehead.

"Just by way of receipt," he murmured, and dashed on.

TALL WINDOWS opened from a balcony of the Grand Central terminal upon the ramp. As Wentworth raced toward them, he glimpsed shadows that sprang from those windows toward the black hulk of a strangely shaped car that waited on the ramp—an armored car! Silent laughter parted the Spider's lips, and the muzzle of the machine-gun swung.

The chatter of the weapon was a muted, faint sound in the thunder of the bedlam that poured out from the concourse, but Wentworth needed no audible proof of his prowess. One of those leaping bodies jerked wildly in mid-air and its limbs were suddenly asprawl. Another was snatched up as his feet struck the ground and pinned back against the stone wall. Three others went down like brittle trees before a hurricane and only a single gun spat flame from the shadow of the armored car.

The muzzle of the machine-gun swerved by three inches, and there was no more pistol flame.

Wentworth dashed toward the armored car, heard faintly the roar of its engine and it lurched forward! In a long leap, he had the door handle in his fist, wrenched at it, and jammed the machine-gun through the opening. No need to shoot. He struck fiercely with the weighted muzzle and a man pitched out from behind the wheel, the truck grated to a halt against the wall. Wentworth was in the narrow crevice between the steel-sided truck and the stone of the building itself, an admirable fortress. He peered fiercely about and for the first time was aware that guns were spitting at him from those windows above. He saw the flame, but the sounds... He tilted up the muzzle of his machine-gun, and it was finished.

This minor skirmish was finished, but the Spider was only beginning! There must be dozens of such crews of looters, unless... unless they had already completed their vicious task and fled! With the thought, Wentworth mounted the side of the truck and stepped across to the sill of the nearest window. It was while he stood there, peering, deafened by the horror within, that the lights went on again. In the same instant, Wentworth's dazzled eyes were aware of stone-dust springing in little geysers from the wall beside him! He crouched, whirled the gun—and saw his assailants! Blue-coated police were swarming along the drive. One of them crouched and began to hose lead from a machine-gun!

Wentworth sprang backward through the window and the air was shrill with the sound of questing lead. Wentworth fell, scrambled to his feet and was aware that he could also hear the cracking of guns... Then the frantic roar of the Falcon's victims was subsiding! Such was the blessing, the benediction of light. In a long stride, Wentworth reached the stone balustrade of the balcony and peered downward upon the hell below. Blue-coated police were swarming in through the doors where the thronged and panic-stricken people had jammed in their efforts at escape. The center of the great concourse was empty... empty of the living. There were sprawled dark forms there, scores of them, a hundred....

Wentworth's furious eyes quested, quested for some sign of the killers, but nowhere was there anyone who wore the helmet of the Falcon—except for himself! Swiftly, Wentworth stripped the helmet off and tossed it aside while his horror-sickened eyes wandered over the pathetic scene below. A woman, crushed by a thousand trampling feet, still held a headless child and yonder was the silvery head of an old man and beside him the form of a woman, close together, together to the end. And there was a golden-haired girl, whose gleaming tresses were horribly stiffened... God, yes, the Falcon had flown this way.

Somewhere a man's voice boomed out, "There is nothing more to fear! The police have taken charge! Be quiet please, and clear the doors so that we can help those who are hurt! Let the doctors in!"

There was a great natural volume to that deep voice and Wentworth's suddenly narrowed eyes went hunting again, with suspicion in their depths... and he remembered the police who were behind him, just outside the high windows. The machine-gun in his hands was useless against them, for the Spider did not, could not, fight against the police. His bullets were only for the criminals, the killers of the world.

Yet he lingered here, while he sought out the man with the deep booming voice. Abruptly, his eyes riveted to the balcony at the other end of the long concourse and his hands gripped the machine-gun until they were rigid and white. For the man who stood on the balcony and sent his calming shouts over the stricken thousands below was a great figure of a man, with bare, fiery red hair! Wentworth knew, even as his eyes took in the speaker, that it was Dacey Hunt, who cried out—Dacey Hunt who was acting as commissioner of the police!

Well, he had wanted to see Dacey Hunt, hadn't he? He had wanted to see if his chest carried the bruise of a saber point that had been turned by a coat of mail! Hunt was the length of the Grand Central away and there were hundreds of police sweeping into the building. Out there, they would find the evidence that the Spider had come this way and his face still bore the make-up of that nemesis of the night! Nor could he escape them by removing the disguise, for Richard Wentworth was equally proscribed tonight. Those things were a glancing thought across his brain, and they did not deter him for a moment. Gripping the machine-gun under his coat, Wentworth turned and began to sprint in a crouch along the balcony, racing toward the red headed giant who was the acting commissioner of the police!

DACEY HUNT'S voice was still booming out to reassure the people below and he was succeeding, he and the blue-coated hordes that poured in through the doors. Drawn back behind him, the dark-haired Vixen stood. Her face was chalk-white and her dark eyes were strained wide. Dacey Hunt turned toward her and smiled grimly.

"Still glad you insisted on coming?" he asked dryly. "Sergeant, get to a phone and order all hospital reserves sent here on a disaster call."

The blue-coated officer saluted and hurried off to obey the

orders and Dacey Hunt was alone with the girl. "A nice haul here tonight," he said, deep-voiced. "Whoever pulled this off must have got away with a couple of hundred thousand dollars."

The Vixen came slowly toward him, her red lips parted now. She threw her arms about his neck and drew his mouth down to hers, passionately... They were were like that when the Spider darted out onto the balcony. He checked and pale fury made points of fire in his eyes. He lifted the machine-gun and sent his flat and mocking laughter at them, sinister, menacing....

"Nero fiddled while Rome burned," came his voice, sibilant and bitter with his anger. "But you rather surpass that, Dacey Hunt."

Hunt's head jerked up and the Vixen whipped from his arms, shrank back while the two men faced each other; Dacey Hunt with his fiery head thrown high and his bold eyes direct, the Spider pale under his make-up and with a machine-gun in his hands.

"Unfasten your coats and your shirt, Hunt," Wentworth ordered curtly. "Hurry, before I open them for you with bullets."

Hunt smiled with a slow and heavy movement of his solid lips. "I think I know who you are," he said quietly, "despite your lack of proper garments. The Spider, isn't it? And why worry about opening up my coats? The bullets will go through."

"Obey, fool!" Wentworth snapped. "If you wear no chain-mail and if there is no bruise over your heart, you go free! If there is...."

Hunt's eyes did not waver.

Wentworth's lipless mouth opened in a smile that was deliberately ugly. "Then I will know certainly what I already am nearly convinced of—that you are the Falcon! That you must die!"

There was a puzzled frown on Hunt's forehead. He opened his lips to speak, shook his head. Wentworth's tautly attuned senses were keeping careful watch. Police might come here at any moment. They might see him from the opposite balcony and shoot, and the girl....

"Stand still," he ordered her softly. "I do not like to hurt women, but I have, at times—when they deserved it."

Her lips were parted in a slight smile and there was that bold, feral strength in her dark eyes. Her breath was quick, jerking at her bodice. Dacey Hunt's eyes swung toward her slowly, glanced at the heavy circlet of gold she wore as a bracelet and his smile widened. There was admiration in his eyes.

"It was cleverly done, Vixen," he said. "Damned clever. So it was passion that made you beat me on the chest with your fists, was it? Beat me so hard that your bracelet made a bruise... Very clever indeed, Vixen." His eyes swung back to the Spider. "There is no need for me to loosen my coats. There is a bruise on my chest, though what it is supposed to mean or who *this* Falcon is that you mention, I have no idea at all. Well, man, get on with it! If you're going to shoot, then *shoot!*"

Wentworth swore softly and his bitter gaze held that of the man before him. He was implying that this girl was in the Falcon's employ and had marked him. Was it clever subterfuge—or was it truth? There was a boldness and a strength in this man, Hunt, that he liked, but the Falcon had those same qualities and his face... Wentworth studied it with the eyes of a man who knows intimately all the tricks of disguise and he knew that Hunt could have been altered to resemble the Falcon. But, damn it, would a red-headed man flaunt that tell-tale flag in the face of his enemy, even when he was sure of killing that enemy?

Wentworth shook his head sharply. He could hear the crisp approach of footsteps now in the echoing vault of the corridor that led to the balcony. It would be one of the police, without a doubt.

"Shoot!" Dacey Hunt jeered.

A thin smile crossed Wentworth's lips. "You are either guilty and clever," he said softly, "or you are a damned brave man, Hunt. I will learn the truth, and… I do not attack the innocent, Hunt. But if you are guilty, God help you, for there will be no place in the world where the man who has perpetrated this night's work can hide!"

Wentworth leaped suddenly forward and Hunt made a swift retreat, threw himself on guard. Wentworth turned aside, threw an arm about Vixen and, tossing her across his shoulder, sprinted for the opposite end of the balcony. His move was so unexpected that he had almost reached the protection of the exit before Hunt recovered himself. He sprang in pursuit then, and his shout to the police rang out fiercely!

THE VIXEN was strangely passive in Wentworth's grip, but he felt her movement, felt her hand reach down toward her knee. His lips shut grimly. So she had a gun there, did she? A deliberate and cool-headed vixen all right. And he could not free a hand. He still needed the machine-gun… He threw everything into a desperate effort to reach the doorway. Hunt's deep voice was tolling the police in pursuit.

"Shoot at his legs!" Hunt ordered. "But be damned careful! And don't let the girl get away!"

A gun crashed out and the bullet gouged up the floor ahead. The Vixen... Wentworth leaped for the door and with the same movement, tossed her from his shoulder. Her high heels struck the floor, but she was off balance. The small automatic in her fist blasted straight up and in an instant, Wentworth wrenched it from her hand. He pivoted then and sent a blast from the machine-gun high over the heads of Hunt and the blue-coated sergeant who had sprung in pursuit. Hunt threw himself prone, ripped the gun from the hand of the sergeant as the man pitched down beside him.

Wentworth fired again, felt a savage blow strike at the back of his neck, the cut of metal. He was half stunned, but he whirled around to catch the Vixen's wrists as she struck again with that heavy bracelet. Her eyes blazed and her lips were drawn tautly back from her teeth. There was no time to fight with her.

His stiffened fingers jabbed the side of her throat. Her face twisted in a nerve-spasm and she went limp against him. Wentworth took her once more over his shoulder, fired a final high burst from the machine-gun and then abandoned it. Bent almost double, he raced along the balcony. Short of capture or death, he would not abandon the curiously named Vixen, for whether Hunt was guilty or an innocent man, there was no doubt that the Vixen was in the employ of the Falcon! Here at last was a thread that he might trace—and at its end? The Spider's mirthless smile distorted his mouth.

To any other man, his position must have seemed hopeless, but Wentworth already had made his plan even in that swift moment when he leaped to capture the Vixen and bear her off from the side of Dacey Hunt himself. The place was encircled by the police, but they would be intent more on helping the stricken than on capturing the Falcon's men, whom they already knew to have escaped. It would take Dacey Hunt a few moments to organize them, and longer still for them to attempt to head him off. Furthermore, they were hampered in shooting for fear of hitting the girl. If he could reach the windows through which he first had entered the Grand Central terminal; if he could recapture the armored car....

Wentworth's laboring breath surged against his locked teeth. Feet were spurning the floor in pursuit and, though the Spider had long trained himself to speed and endurance, burdened as he was it was not likely that he could long out—distance the men behind him. He could not shoot....

His eyes combed the way ahead. There was a door there where the balcony ended in a corridor. If it were not locked now, and if he could pass it, secure it from the other side... Wentworth lengthened his stride, heard guns begin to speak behind him again; slow, careful shots, aimed at his flying legs. Along the opposite balcony, the police were racing to head him off. He had a lead of seventy-five yards over them; no more than that and they were unburdened. Behind him... but Wentworth could not spare even the split-second it would take to glance back. The door was very close. If he could pass that….

Wentworth threw everything into the final effort to reach that door, but with a haunting fear in the back of his mind. If it was locked… His hand was outstretched before him to seize that knob at the first possible moment. He would need every split moment of time. His hand touched the big bronze knob, gripped and turned. His quick eyes had seen that the door opened toward him and he checked and threw his weight into a backward heave. The knob turned all right, but the door didn't move. The door… Dear God, *the door was locked!* And he had acknowledged to Dacey Hunt that he was the Spider!

Wentworth whirled while his haunted eyes swept the balcony rail, the floor a dozen yards below, the police racing along the opposite balcony and the half-dozen men charging down with ready guns, with triumphant shouts on their lips. Trapped.

CHAPTER 7
FRIEND OF DEATH

EVEN AS the police raced to the capture, Wentworth decried a faint hope. Those same high windows also lined this balcony, but they were high and the girl… Despair darkened Wentworth's eyes. There was no other way. With an oath of disappointment, he dumped the girl to the floor against the wall and, with the release of her weight, leaped instantly for the windowsill. His hands clutched its edge and all the lithe strength of his body went into a frantic upward surge. His shoul-

IRON MIKE

DACEY HUNT

der muscles bulged, seemed to crack. Breath gusted explosively from his lips but his upward heave let his knees grip the sill. Headlong, an elbow bent over his head, other hand raking out before him, he went forward into the deep recess of the window.

Guns were crashing out below. There was a stunning burn across his thighs, the wicked whine of ricocheting lead, then he could draw his legs, too, into the embrasure. But there was no security here, save for that instant. As soon as those sprinting police across the width of the concourse reached an opposite position they could pour their lead into his helpless body. Wentworth had calculated to perfection. As he drew his legs up under him, he thrust himself backward at the window. The glass bulged, burst under the pressure and, batting at a threatening shard with his coated forearm, he climbed out on the narrow ledge that skirted the building. A dozen feet below was the circling driveway of the ramp. He saw policemen climbing toward the railing from the street below, but for the moment he was safe.

With a deliberate calm, he felt his way along the ledge until

MARTIN WOLF

MOIRE SHOVIC

he could reach the next windowsill... beyond that locked door. He reached it as the police were scrambling over the railing of the ramp. He pushed through the glass, dropped to the floor inside. It was an exhibit room, walled off from the open pit of the concourse and he was secure from the guns of the men opposite—secure from all of them until they should follow in his footsteps from window to window. Before that time... A grim smile touched Wentworth's lips. There was a rolled fire hose in the corner, fastened to a water outlet. And on the other side of the door was the Vixen....

In a leap, Wentworth had seized the hose and was twisting the valve wheel. Water surged through the tubing, making it writhe in his hands as he sprang to the door and whipped it open. Whatever the police were expecting, it was not his return by way of that door. A frantic shout ripped from the lips of the leading man, now almost reaching the window, then the stream of the high-pressure water caught him in the face and bowled him backward. A sweep of the nozzle and the remaining five men, including the huge figure of Dacey Hunt, were hammered from their feet, sent rolling and sprawling by the powerful stream.

In an instant, Wentworth had seized the Vixen and dragged her through into the room, slammed the door with its spring lock. He jammed the nozzle between two exhibit cases, trained on the window through which he had broken, and once more he was racing away from his pursuers... with his captive secure again.

The exhibit room ran to the west end of the building and

there was a window there. It would not be over the armored car by half the depth of the terminal, but Wentworth could reach it without exposing himself and his captive to the erratic gunfire of the police. He clambered to the sill while bullets began to punch at the locked door behind him. They would be looking for him in front of the station and there was just a chance… He eased up the window and peered out cautiously. Except for a single guard beside the armored truck, there was not a person in sight!

Wentworth ducked back inside again and bent swiftly over the Vixen, lifted her so that she appeared to lean out the window, and he softened his voice to a whisper.

"Officer!" he called softly. "Oh, officer, please help me! There's shooting out here and… and I'm afraid!"

He made small effort to imitate a woman's tones other than to lighten his voice, for a whisper is almost impossible of identification. For a moment, the officer hesitated, then he came at a run. "Just you take it easy, Miss," he called, "and you'll be all right. Just take it easy…."

When he was directly under the window, Wentworth lifted the Vixen so that she sat with her legs hanging outside on the sill. "I'm going to jump!" he whispered. "I'm going to jump!"

The officer braced himself, held up his hands and Wentworth dropped the Vixen carefully the few yards into his arms. The next instant, while the bewildered policeman held an unconscious girl, Wentworth dropped beside him and swung a carefully calculated blow to the jaw. It was easy after that. A quick dash, a few moments to bind the Vixen, who was beginning to regain consciousness, and then the heavy armored truck began to roll... and the man behind the wheel wore a police uniform cap, taken from the guard!

WENTWORTH MADE no effort at haste. He waved a hand as he went past the police who were crowding across the roadway of the ramp. Moments later, he was rolling down lower Park Avenue toward security, and he hoped, toward the defeat of the Falcon! The Vixen was glowering at him now with venomous eyes and the Spider turned a brief, cold smile upon her.

"Not quite the ending for the evening that you had planned, was it?" he asked.

"It will end all right," the Vixen said softly, with a clipped ferocity to her words. "It will end with your death!"

Wentworth peered forward through the windshield and the smile dwindled from his lips. "Perhaps," he acknowledged quietly.

Now that the push of action was over, his mind could race ahead to the plans he had laid. He had, actually, accomplished nothing toward the defeat of the Falcon's plans; he was as much in doubt as ever as to the possibility that Dacey Hunt was the criminal. He had only *this* captive who definitely was connected with the Falcon—but there was one difficulty. The Spider could compel himself to resort to any necessary means to make a man talk; or he could convince the man of that fact. The Vixen wouldn't scare worth a damn!

There was no time even to question her now, actually, for if Dacey Hunt were the Falcon, Wentworth knew that his challenge tonight, the fact that he had even suspected the man, increased the dangers of Stanley Kirkpatrick, the stricken commissioner of police, by many hundred fold. Hunt would know—supposing him to be the Falcon—that the Spider would lose no time in communicating his doubts to Kirkpatrick… Instantly, his course sprang clearly into his mind.

Five blocks to the east, crowded in behind tenement buildings, Wentworth had a private garage with another such car as he had been forced to abandon uptown. There would be weapons there and the materials of disguise. If he escaped observation when he entered, he would be able to lodge *this* stolen truck, and his prisoner, there until he could have time to devise a use for the Vixen, or a means to make her talk. Afterward, he must make all haste to Kirkpatrick's quarters.

The exchange of cars was swiftly effected and Wentworth left the vindictive Vixen, bound and gagged, in the rear of the garaged truck. He wrapped her warmly against the cold of the night, though in this sheltered spot, and within the truck, she was well protected.

"I wouldn't toss about too much if I were you, Vixen," he told her with a slight, chill smile. "It's apt to be cold before morning."

The Vixen's dark eyes glared at him above the gag, but she made no other sign that she had heard and Wentworth locked the garage and drove off. He took the time, on a back street, to remove all evidences of his disguise and to straighten out his clothing, renewed from a hidden store in the garage.

For it would be Richard Wentworth, who went to call on Kirkpatrick—Richard Wentworth who was being hunted for murder… Dispassionately, he surveyed himself in the make-up mirror, estimating his fatigue and remaining reserves from the tired, taut lines about his mouth and the weariness of his eyes. He must rest soon or pay the penalty in slowed reactions and blunted mind, a difference that might mean life or death to the Spider! Rest? How could he hope to rest when this fresh scourge was lashing humanity? He had fought so hard tonight, and so futilely, and the Falcon... the Falcon had slaughtered, and won! THE SICK remembrance of that shambles amid the happy holiday crowd at Grand Central preyed upon his nerves and, for the first time, as he tooled his way steadily northward toward the apartment town-home of Kirkpatrick, he could turn his mind to some of the mysteries he had witnessed. There had been nothing puzzling about that first appearance of the hawk-figure at the window of Iron Mike's bit house, nor about the murder of the Mug that had followed. It had seemed to Wentworth a straightforward affair of smashing in a man's skull with a club. Now, he was not so sure.

Among the slain at the terminal had been many whose heads had been horribly shattered and he had seen the taxi driver die... under the attack of a *Shadow!* Wild conjecture swept Wentworth's brain. The Falcon's name, the scream of the hawk, brought to immediate mind the idea of huge hawks, trained to strike at human beings....

Wentworth shook his head sharply. Nothing smaller than an eagle could strike with such force, and the eagle did not strike with the clenched fist as some falcons did. It seized with inch-long talons.

Wentworth frowned, shook his head. A falcon, of course, struck with the force of a swoop that might range up to a hundred feet... but, damn it, a falcon did not fly at night and in darkness! What hellish death-weapon had this man, who called himself the Silver Falcon, devised for the torment of humanity? Wentworth shook the puzzle from his weary brain. It could not be answered now. Time, time was needed, and it might be drawing so damnably short. Slumped down behind the wheel in an attempt at relaxation, Wentworth knew again the goad of despair.

The thought of Nita came to him as a fresh torment. Before his eyes, her sweet face with its loyal eyes and the proud crown of chestnut hair floated like a mirage of water in a thirsty desert. God! She, too, had been stricken by this madman, carried off to some private asylum of the Falcon's own selection and domination, according to his boast. Wentworth had not even been able to initiate inquiries about her. Would the police listen to a man accused of murder and his cry of frame-up? Would they believe his story of Nita's abduction? If Kirkpatrick were in charge, they might. But with him ill, and Dacey Hunt in the saddle, there was no chance. Wentworth did not even know the fate of his faithful servitors, Jackson and the warrior Sikh, Ram Singh. Perhaps, Kirkpatrick might help there....

Two blocks from the Fifth Avenue apartment house in which Kirkpatrick lived, Wentworth parked his car and hurried on afoot. There were guns beneath his arms again but they could not help a despairing heart... Entering the apartment building was a routine matter. Wentworth did not dare use the main door, but there was a service entrance whose lock yielded readily to the tools and skill of the Spider and afterward, he climbed long flights of steps until he stood outside the service door of Kirkpatrick's apartment. He used the lock-pick again, stepped inside... and light blazed into his eyes.

In the kitchen doorway stood a small, bathrobe-swaddled figure with a neat, black automatic in his palm—a small man with the slanted almond eyes of the Orient, and an impassive face. When he recognized Wentworth, something like a smile brightened his eyes and he tucked the gun back into his sleeve, bowed politely.

"Wentworth, *san,*" he said gently. "The master have wish you come."

Wentworth's own lips relaxed in a slight smile, "Thank you, Lee Chang," he said. "Is Kirkpatrick *san* awake?"

Lee Chang bowed and led the way on soundless feet along a brief service corridor, across a dining room, a bachelor's comfortable drawing-room and into another corridor where the dim beam of a night-light shone through a doorway.

"Nurse have gone sleep," Lee Chang whispered. "Master *there!*"

He indicated the room where the light shone and Wentworth, his face serious, a frown between his keen eyes, stepped across the sill; and he fought to keep the sudden alarm from showing on his mobile lips. Kirkpatrick lay flat in the bed without even a pillow and with his feet propped higher than his head. When Wentworth entered, his friend's head turned with a weighted slowness. There was feverishness in the heavy eyes and a tinge of blue touched the lips—the only color in his saturnine, drawn face. Those lips moved slightly, a smile.

"Hello, Dick," he whispered.

WENTWORTH HAD expected to find Kirkpatrick ill, but this was death! Anger flooded his brain. Hell damn the Falcon, who had done this to an able and powerful man! He had said Kirkpatrick would die in a week, but from the look of him, it was a thing that might come at any moment.

Wentworth reached the bed in a stride, stood with his fingers biting into Kirkpatrick's shoulder. They had been close friends, had faced death together many times—and as the Spider and the commissioner of police, they had fought, though Kirkpatrick had never been able to prove Wentworth's guilt. So they lived and worked in a wary truce; and they were such friends as only strong men of fierce integrity can be. Wentworth felt a pain like cold poison eating at his heart. Poison… That was what had done *this* thing to Kirkpatrick.

Wentworth pulled up a chair and, in that quiet moment, he had made up his mind. Kirkpatrick must know the truth, and the complete truth. A weaker man might die under the shock of that, but Wentworth felt that it would strengthen Kirkpatrick. Something must, or he would die!

"Lee Chang," Wentworth said quietly. "I want you to hear this. Your master has not had a heart attack. He has been poisoned."

The dullness that seemed to sheathe Kirkpatrick's eyes lifted for a moment and the keen blade of his will flashed through. "Poisoned?" His voice was stronger. "But that fool doctor—a Doctor Martin Wolf—who happened to be in headquarters… How do you know, Dick?"

Wentworth caught at Kirkpatrick's phrase about the doctor called Martin Wolf and his eyes narrowed in sharp thought. Somehow, the Falcon had managed to introduce poison into Kirkpatrick's food at some restaurant. That would be easy enough, probably, by substituting one of his men for a waiter, either through bribery or force. Then knowing about when the poison would strike, he had arranged to have a physician on hand who would take charge of Kirkpatrick!

But he could not question the weakened Kirkpatrick about that. Instead he explained how he surmised poisoning and described the events of the night. He made no mention of Nita's kidnaping, nor of the murder charge against himself of which Kirkpatrick palpably had no knowledge. Kirkpatrick's attention must not be diverted to issues such as that; he would need all his will and concentration to fight for life....

While Wentworth talked, Kirkpatrick lay with closed eyes, so still that death seemed already to have mastered him, but the quickened lift of his chest told of his attention. Wentworth's hand rested lightly on his friend's wrist, feeling the thready, rapid pulse. He looked across the sick bed at Lee Chang.

"Lee Chang," he ordered softly, "you will throw out everything in the house that could possibly be poisoned: medicine, tobacco, toothpaste, all foodstuffs and liquors—even those which you feel sure could not have been tampered with. This nurse must go—the doctor be changed."

Kirkpatrick signified with a quickened gesture of his hand that he agreed and there was a slight frown between his eyes, but it did not endure. He was too prostrated even to be able to concentrate on the problem of his own survival. Wentworth had come with the firm intention of carrying Kirkpatrick to safer quarters, to the home perhaps of the Spider's own physician, but one glance showed that the transfer would be impossible. Kirkpatrick was too weak.

Wentworth nodded and, despite the peril of each passing moment here and the driving need to renew his warfare with the Falcon, he stayed on to await the arrival of his own hurriedly summoned doctor. Kirkpatrick fell presently into an exhausted sleep and, with Lee Chang, Wentworth strode to the nurse's room, jarred the woman awake and made his accusation... but learned nothing. His first thought had been to send her away at once, but now a new idea presented itself. He called Lee Chang....

"Maybe so *this* woman help poison Kirkpatrick *san*," Wentworth said. "I'm not sure. Maybe so this strange doctor who came home with Kirkpatrick *san* helped poison him. Maybe so you can keep Doctor Martin Wolf and the nurse here until I come again?"

Lee Chang smiled with a slight wrinkling of his parchment-like face. "Can do," he said mildly.

Wentworth's own fine smile answered him. A few hours of imprisonment and fright might help loosen the nurse's tongue. The doctor... Wentworth thought he might use a bit of pressure on that gentleman!

WHEN WENTWORTH'S physician, Dr. Bradley, arrived, Kirkpatrick was still deep in sleep and they did not rouse him, but Dr. Bradley agreed to remain on the spot.

"You're pretty close to the ragged edge yourself, Dick," Dr. Bradley growled. "How long do you think you can keep up this mad pace? Never sleeping! Never resting! Driving yourself to the brink of exhaustion! Your heart is going to crack wide open one of these days and that will be the finish for you. That's what will do it, not bullets."

Wentworth smiled slightly, but graveness crowded the expression from his lips. "Perhaps," he acknowledged. "Doc, I want you to get me a list of every private sanitarium in the state, in Jersey and Connecticut—the 'nerve' sanitariums where they imprison the insane."

"I think that would be excellent," Bradley agreed dryly. "We might force you to rest by putting you in a strait-jacket, in a padded cell with two guards."

Wentworth's face twitched and his eyes darkened. Nita might be... like that! He spoke heavily, "Nita has been kidnaped and, according to the threat, put in a sanitarium."

Bradley swore harshly, instantly muted his voice. "God, Dick! I didn't know. Can't the police... Of course, I remember now. You've been framed and Jackson and Ram Singh have been arrested as accessories...."

Wentworth's lips tightened at *this* fresh disaster, but he had more than expected it. He scarcely heard Bradley's prompt promise to get the information about sanitariums as soon as the state offices opened.

He clasped Bradley's hand warmly, turned toward the service exit. Already, he had lost too much time and so much remained to be done....

In the kitchen Lee Chang was resolutely emptying his shelves of all foodstuffs. He bobbed in a low bow.

"My knowing everything be all right you come, Wentworth *san*," he said. "My thanking you, Wentworth *san*."

The Chinese's words lingered in Wentworth's mind pleasantly as he hurried out by the route he had used to enter, and they made a warm glow about his heart. It did not strike him as incongruous, that a servant's words of gratitude should fall so gratefully upon his ears. The Spider spent his entire life and fortune in the service of the people—yet gratitude was so rare that when it came it buoyed him for days. Sad commentary upon the humanity of the people he served! But Wentworth did not ask gratitude. The work itself was recompense enough and the knowledge that a criminal had been brought to justice....

THE HAGGARD dawn surprised Wentworth when he stepped out into the biting cold of the street. So much time had sped... so little was accomplished. He reviewed in his mind the plans that he had formed hours ago, before he could have guessed at such horror as had struck in Grand Central—a device by which he hoped to avert a repetition of disaster in the promised raid tomorrow upon the Metropole Museum! But it was already *today!* He turned up his coat collar against the cold, which his fatigue accentuated, and walked rapidly toward his car....

"The other aerie," the Falcon had cried when the Mug had been killed. Surely, those words implied that the bit house of Iron Mike was the only other headquarters of the killers he had drawn about him?

91

Wentworth stumbled and swayed off balance as he climbed into the parked car and his lips thinned at the recognition of his exhaustion. Still there could be no rest… He took up his thoughts again, deliberately. Iron Mike was exactly such a huge, powerful man as the Falcon had proved to be, and his high voice might be a deliberate falsification of tone to conceal the deep rumble of the Falcon. For the rest, disguise could take care of it. Wentworth's eyes narrowed. His plan called for the imprisonment of Iron Mike and the rest of the Falcon's killers. He would give Iron Mike a perfect alibi—then see if the Falcon himself appeared!

Simple as was Wentworth's plan, it called for skill and incredible strain for a man wearied as he was by hours of battle and mental torture. Simple, yes! He planned to loot a federal seizure of drugs and plant the narcotics in the bit house where Iron Mike and the rest couldn't find them—but where the federal men, whom presently Wentworth would inform, would *inevitably* discover them! With his killers in jail, with Iron Mike himself out of the way, the Spider would see whether the Falcon could stage his museum raid!

Grimly, while the pale light of the winter dawn streaked the sky, Richard Wentworth once more drew out a make-up tray and, with the skill of long practice, rapidly transformed his face. If he failed in his coming venture, there would be nothing about him to point the finger of infamy at Richard Wentworth, or at the Spider! He would be just another nameless criminal fallen before the guns of the law….

For a moment, as he worked, a pang of heartache twitched at

Wentworth's breast. If he failed, what would become of Nita? Of his faithful servitors, Jackson and Ram Singh, imprisoned by the police?

Wentworth thrust the thoughts from his brain, lest his unwavering courage be shaken; lest they should weaken him at a critical moment. More than that, his fears could not do, for the Spider served a cause, and before *that* command all human frailties—even all human sentiments—must give way!

CHAPTER 8
INTO THE TRAP

WENTWORTH KNEW well where the federals stored the narcotics they seized. In his long career as an amateur criminologist, he had had dealings with government agencies as well as the police—and he knew that the federals counted more on the awe of criminals than on any intrinsic strength of their storage vaults to protect the drugs. Not that the plan on which Wentworth had launched himself was without danger. Far from it! There were men on duty in the federal building at all hours and mere discovery there would earn the Spider's death at the hands of expert marksmen! And once that first step was accomplished, he must face the problem of planting the stolen drugs in the bit house.

In the end, Wentworth determined to trust wholly to his speed and skill with safes and locks. He reached the federal building by the familiar process of crossing roofs and climbing the barriers of pointed steel which interposed—not too difficult for a man of the Spider's cool nerves. Once there, he arranged his web so that he could swiftly drop to a high window; then he created a diversion for which he had carefully prepared. He made sure the street was entirely empty of people and tossed a hand grenade fairly on the steps of the federal building!

Wentworth did not wait to see the results. He was gambling that the blast would pull every man in the building to the windows or the street and hold them there for a few minutes. If it failed… Grimly, Wentworth took no account of failure. He could not. No sooner had the grenade left his hand than he had sprung to the silken rope, swung over the rear of the building. The first rolling crash of the explosion was lashing across the district, smashing out windows and drawing out the startled shouts of men, when Wentworth slid down the rope and dangled just beside a window. He broke it while glass still tinkled from other shattered panes, and sprang inside the building. He knew precisely where he was going and what he must do; he raced along a dimly lit corridor. Speed was everything… and his skill did not desert him in his need for haste.

Two minutes after the blast, and while the furious federal agents still combed the streets, Wentworth had opened the safe. Swiftly, he stuffed a bag he carried with packages of narcotic powders, several hundred thousand dollars worth, then raced for the roof. As he neared the office by which he had entered, a man popped into sight in the corridor, stared at him, grabbed for a gun… Wentworth hurled the close-packed bag at his face and dived in right behind it. While the man staggered off balance from the solid blow dealt by the loaded bag, Wentworth lashed out with an iron-hard fist and put him out, cold. Thereafter, it was only a matter of reclimbing the dangling silken rope and retracing his steps across the roofs.

It was touch and go for a few moments when he reached the street. A radio patrolman who had answered the bomb alarm spotted him, flung up his gun and ordered the Spider to halt! Wentworth answered by tossing a tear-gas bomb at the cop's feet and running at top speed toward his own car... A half hour later, Blinky McQuade presented himself at Iron Mike's bit house with a large, newspaper-wrapped bundle under his arm. Mike himself did not come to the door, and Wentworth did not know the man who opened it narrowly to inspect him. However, his keen eyes, hidden by Blinky's hooded spectacles, detected at once that the man recognized him! There was an involuntary tightening of the flesh about the eyes and a gleam of hatred, instantly masked. As the door was swung wide to admit him, Wentworth hid his discovery and stalked forward, grumbling curses under his breath.

"Take your time opening the door," he mumbled. "Take your time. It's only Blinky McQuade and he don't count for nothing no more. But you watch your step. You watch your step. Wait until Iron Mike gets here..." He wheeled sharply toward the lanky, sharp-boned man who let him in. "When's Iron Mike coming?" he demanded harshly. "Eh? When's he coming?"

"None of your damned business, Blinky!" The man grinned at him with a thin, evil twisting of his lips. "You'll find out!"

Wentworth pretended not to take alarm, but a glimpse of

the man's face had told him as surely as if the words had been shouted aloud in his ear: *The Spider had walked into a trap!*

WELL, HE had expected that, hadn't he? After the Mug had been killed, the life of the man who had talked to him was equally forfeit. Yes, Blinky McQuade could expect danger here, but if he could find a way to leave his newspaper bundle here and then quit the place....

There was a hard smile in Wentworth's own eyes. He ignored the few greetings that were called out to him as he also did the hostile stares of other men in the room. He slumped down at a table and rasped an order for a drink.

Under the cover of his spectacles, his eyes made a rapid circuit of the room. He caught covert glances exchanged among certain of the crooks present. Would they strike at once, or wait until they communicated with the Falcon himself? Wentworth unbuttoned his coat, turned down the collar—and freed the holsters under his arms. If they attacked at once, they would not find the Spider unprepared! Minutes crept past. A few of the men made conspicuously casual exits, getting ready! Wentworth hid a smile as he pretended to toss off the filthy liquor that was served in the bit house. They had waited too long! He lurched to his feet and, imitating the half-blind shuffle of Blinky McQuade, stumped toward the washroom with the newspaper bundle tucked under his arm....

Once the door closed behind him, Wentworth sprang into action. He half-emptied the wastebasket there—the first time anything had been removed from it in months—and tucked his newspaper bundle under the debris. With other papers, he rapidly made a bundle of some of the trash, and his task was performed. He need only escape, phone the narcotics office of the federal enforcement agency... and the bit-house customers and Iron Mike would be poured into cells! Wentworth smiled, moved toward the door and it was then he heard the sound.

It was very faint. Probably a real Blinky McQuade would not have heard it, but the Spider knew his danger and he had been on the alert for the first hint of attack. It was no more than a whisper, the faint shuffle of feet and a furtive order. But he knew instantly that the ambush was arranged. There were men in the hall just outside the door!

Wentworth flung a sharp glance about him. The window... Yes, he could escape by that route, but a second thought told him that such a slipping-away would foredoom his plan. No, he had to play out the role of Blinky McQuade—and he had to let them see him escape with that bundle of useless newspaper under his arm, no matter at what cost!

One thing Wentworth could do. He drew a gun from its holster and tucked it among the newspapers, gripped it in his fist as he moved toward the door. He began grumbling to himself, flung it open and stepped out into the darkness of the hall. Instantly, he saw the half-dozen gunmen assembled there, and made his swift estimate of the possibilities while, *apparently*, he was still in ignorance of the ambuscade.

"Just a minute, Blinky!"

Wentworth whipped about, a startled cry in his throat, to confront the thin man who had welcomed him at the door of the bit house. Now for the first time he seemed aware of the men, saw the dangling, but ready, guns in their fists. He made no move toward his own holsters, though the automatic snouted toward his enemies under the cover of the newspaper bundle.

"Hey! What the hell is this?" He made his voice frightened, quavering.

"We just want a little talk with you, Blinky," the thin man said gently. "Just a little talk with you about things—for old time's sake. Step down to the office, won't you?"

Wentworth's eyes shuttled over the men in the narrow hallway. They were spread out so that the corridor was blocked in both directions—but so that they could shoot at him without endangering one another. He could break that up in a moment, by a forward spring while he shot down his challenger. But that would be too clever for Blinky McQuade....

"Sure," he said hoarsely. "Sure, I'll go to the office with you. Iron Mike want to see me?"

The man laughed, and the sound was little above a whisper. "Sure. Sure, Iron Mike wants to see you! *You go first.*"

WENTWORTH MADE his shoulders cringe. He spun around to face the man and backed along the hallway while he spilled out placating words, incoherent words. Was this where the rub-out was to take place? Or would they want to question him first? He hugged the bundle, with the automatic leveled at the chest of the leader. The man was pacing after him, step by step, but he left a clear lane of fire for the other men.

There was a light on the wall behind Wentworth and it threw pale gleams across the killers' faces that grinned at him like the gaping jaws of hungry wolves. It was murder all right that they intended—murder of a cringing, helpless, half-blind man....

There was a doorway beside Wentworth and he saw the guns coming up, saw them ready. The leader would fire first, of course, and from him there would be no warning at all. A twist of the wrist and flame and lead spitting from his gun... Wentworth drew in a soft breath caught the hardening glitter of the leader's eyes and knew that the moment had come.

"We'll talk here, Blinky," he said, and his gun wrist tautened into movement!

Wentworth squeezed the trigger of his gun and the recoil of the blast seemed to blow him sideways into that doorway. The blast of the gun was incredible in that narrow hallway, and it was the one thing on which the killers hadn't counted. They would not guess that Blinky had a heavy gun or that its lead, striking at a range of less than six feet, would hurl their leader's dying body back upon them. It was true their guns racketed out as if that blast had jarred them into action... but the Spider had shot carefully, and he knew the impact of .45 caliber bullets.

Deliberately, with that shot, he hurled the thin man back upon the guns of his companions and their murderous lead slammed into his skeleton body, bent and twisted it, tumbled it lifeless upon the floor. The light stayed on just long enough for them to realize the shock of the thing they had done, and then it cracked out with Wentworth's second shot.

Afterward, there was darkness in that corridor and a silence that rang with the aftermath of those crashing guns. Half-stunned by the multiple concussion, they didn't even know that

Wentworth had ducked through the doorway and closed the barrier behind him; that while they stood, shaken with the unexpectedness of the thing that had happened, he was ducking out a window and sliding down a doubled strand of the silken web to the ground. When finally, they began to rake the darkness with their lead, there was no target for them to hit.

Grim-lipped, Wentworth doubled away through the drab grayness of the early winter day which seemed only to intensify the sunless darkness of the back courts and narrow alleys. There could be no question now of delay; of waiting for Iron Mike to enter the bit house. The alarm would have to be given at once, before those killers recovered themselves sufficiently to carry the murdered man's body away. They would not hurry too much, because they knew those gunshots would not be reported to the police. In these environs, when a man heard a gunshot, he ran and hid. It was the safer way....

So, from a pay station a half dozen blocks away, Wentworth phoned in his tip-off to the narcotic squad from whom he had stolen the drugs, now safely planted in the washroom waste-basket of the bit house. He told them where to look—and then Blinky McQuade vanished. In his place was the hawk-faced Spider, though divested of cape and broad-rimmed black hat. He drove slowly through the deserted streets and into the tenement court where, in the private garage, he had hidden the armored loot car of the Falcon, with the Vixen a fast prisoner inside.

He would have a use for her presently; in a few hours, too, he would have a list of the sanitariums to which Nita might have been carried a prisoner. But right now... rest. With the end of the sustaining excitement, Wentworth knew that he had driven himself to the breaking-point. There was a numbness in his brain. He stumbled into the garage, glanced briefly at the helpless Vixen, and flung himself down on the front seat of the armored car to sleep....

HE HAD done no more than jerk at the knots of the Vixen's bonds and rearrange the disturbed blankets which he had thrown over her for warmth. He had not noticed the contorted position into which she had twisted herself nor, just beneath the hem of her skirt, the glimmer of steel! Even if he had missed these things, he should have noticed the despairing gleam of the Vixen's eyes as he bent over her, and the exultation as, worn with fatigue, he straightened afterward and dropped down to rest.

The Vixen lay utterly motionless through long seconds, but she need not have concerned herself. The Spider was already and genuinely asleep... When she was sure of that, the Vixen renewed her long hours of effort to reach the knife at her garter.

It had been necessary for her first to gain some leeway in her bonds and that was no easy matter after the masterly job the Spider had done. She had still found it impossible—thanks to the fact that she was also tied to a ring-bolt in the floor—to reach the knife. She had been forced to the long task of working the knife free of her garter so that it would fall on the floor within reach of her tied hands. The blankets in which Wentworth had wrapped her anew further hindered her efforts, but she was persistent, driven hard by both hatred and fear. And in the end—it was nearly two hours later—she got her trembling, numbed fingers upon the knife!

There was then the difficulty of sawing through her bonds, the pain of restoring circulation to deadened feet and hands. Her closely pressed lips gave no evidence of the agony as she waited, but her fingers toyed with the knife which she could not yet surely control. It would not be long now; a few minutes more and her grip upon the hilt would be positive and strong. There was a greedy coldness in her eyes as they riveted on Wentworth's throat, almost within reach of that keen blade... When her hands should be strong enough! She flexed her fingers, massaged her wrists. The knife caught a vagrant gleam of light, cold, merciless.

Wild animals have a faculty that is given to few human beings. Bred on constant peril of their lives, they learn to sleep lightly, nervously, with senses attuned to the approach of danger. An ominous scent in the dark, the lightest hint of a footfall can snap them instantly from sleep, ready for flight or battle. But not always—even the most alert of them fail and are killed....

Richard Wentworth had lived and slept in continuous peril through many years, and it may be that he had acquired some small part of such alertness. It was a fact that he never slept at his home with a gun immediately under his hand lest, being startled from sleep, he injure someone. But this winter day, his energies were at low ebb; his strength drained by long hours of frantic life-and-death struggle; by worry. Certain it is that, as the Vixen at last drew her feet beneath her and rose with the knife lifting in a sure hand, the Spider did not stir.

She was ready now, her strength completely restored. The keen point, the slashing edge… She knew where to strike. She could see the quick pulsing of blood through the carotid there in the side of the Spider's throat It made a faint quivering of the tanned, healthy skin. A slash there would mean death within two minutes at the most, and long before that time Wentworth would be drained of the strength to fight. Was that fast enough? But she did not dare risk a thrust through the clothing into the heart. Something might turn the point and there would be no time for a second stroke. She would drive through the throat, into the seat, hope to pin the dying Spider down, or to slice into the spinal column—and hurl herself flat on the floor.

Her dark eyes were wide and there were hot, eager lights in their depths. Her tongue flicked out and wet the soft, full redness of her mouth. She drew herself up straight, arm lifted high, her whole body tense for the utmost concentration of effort. Her breath made a slight hissing noise between her teeth as she drove the knife down!

Slight as that sound was, it made a sharp break in the contracted silence of the armored truck. It penetrated the Spider's slumbering consciousness… but the knife was already driving down with all the wiry strength of the Vixen's body! What happened then was the result of no deliberate response on the part of the Spider. He could not have opened his eyes, grasped the danger, and avoided it. He heard a sound—and to the Spider any sound spelled peril!

His body jerked while his hand whipped blindly toward a gun; and that jerk was the beginning of an instinctive roll away

103

from the sound that had stabbed into his slumbering senses. He had time to move no more than three inches—but it was enough. The knife hissed past his throat so close that it burned the flesh and its point crunched, inches deep, into the wood of the seat on which he lay.

The next instant the Spider's blindly outflung arm struck the Vixen across the breast and drove her violently backward. She lost her footing, fell over... and Wentworth, his eyes barely open, was on his feet with a heavy automatic cradled in his fist. He saw her then, whipped a glance toward the seat and the remembered sound of crunching wood, and saw the half-buried knife. And the Spider laughed, in spite of the cold perspiration that sprang on his forehead, in spite of the glittering hatred in the Vixen's eyes as slowly, cringingly, she picked herself up off the floor.

"A good try, Vixen," Wentworth said quietly and laughed again at the hint of a tremor in his voice. It was not the nearness of his escape from death that shook him, but the vehemence of the rage in the woman's eyes, and the cold fury which had driven her to strike so murderously at a sleeping man. "A very good try," he repeated, and now his voice was entirely clear, his eyes smiling, too. "I have you to thank for waking me. It's time you and I went about our business."

Vigor was flowing through his veins again. So short a rest, completely relaxed, had given him the recuperation that most men would have needed days to attain. Such were the results of the rigorous training upon which he insisted for himself. He holstered his gun and, with a sharp thrust of his heel, broke the knife off short in the wood. He caught up the hilt with its two jagged inches of steel and moved toward the Vixen, motionless against the locked steel doors at the rear of the car.

"There was a time," he said softly, "when I might have hesitated to do what was necessary to make you talk but you can't expect me to show you any consideration now, can you, because of your sex? Perhaps, it won't even be necessary to hurt you much. A few slashes about the face with the jagged end of the dagger. Not too painful, but I rather think the effects would be permanent. The scars, that is...."

THE VIXEN tried a smile, but it was stiff and ugly on her mouth and there was no color at all in her cheeks. She drew herself up with an attempt at pride. Wentworth did not speak again. He knew the weakness of talking; and knew that the Vixen would recognize it. True killers do not talk of what they are about to do; any more than a wild beast would warn its intended prey.

The bluff had to work, for Wentworth knew that he could not carry it through. He was glad that the face he wore was the merciless mask of the Spider; glad that the Vixen knew he had witnessed the slaughter in Grand Central and blamed her, in part, for that brutal execution. And there were wild rumors in the Underworld about the Spider, legends that had sprung up around his name and exploits. No, the Vixen could not doubt that the Spider would torture her!

He sprang suddenly, seized her and forced her flat upon the floor. An involuntary cry sprang to her lips, then she set her teeth, and forced the smile. Despite his knowledge of the woman's connection with the Falcon and slaughter, Wentworth knew an admiration for her courage that he could not dispel, but he ruled it out of his cold blue-gray eyes, and reached for her mouth with the jagged tip of the blade.

"First the lower lip," Wentworth muttered.

The hard touch of the steel brought a gasp from the Vixen. Her eyes flew wide so that the whites showed entirely around the iris and she wrenched her head aside. The violence of her own movement made a minute scratch, more painful than a deep cut. Wentworth forced out a harsh laugh.

"Now the upper lip!" he said.

"No, no! In God's name!" The Vixen whimpered. "I'll talk. I'll... *talk!*"

The knife hovered over her face and she pleaded. Wentworth knew that he himself was pale. This was violently distasteful to him, but the end justified it—the capture of the Falcon... The Vixen was pleading now.

"Oh, just tell me what you want to know, and if I can... I'll... Do you want to know how to find the Falcon? I can find out. Who he is? I know one of his names! It's Martin Wolf!"

Wentworth smiled slightly—and on the lipless mouth of the Spider it was sinister in the extreme. She had started out by lying. Martin Wolf was the name of a doctor who had been at headquarters when Kirkpatrick was stricken—who had taken Kirkpatrick home. Wentworth's eyes narrowed. Was it possible that the Falcon had exposed himself in such a way; had returned and been imprisoned by Lee Chang according to his orders?

Wentworth shook his head angrily. That wasn't possible... Doubt lingered. But the Vixen said she could find the Falcon.

That was more important just now. Wentworth had made his plans for the Vixen. He intended to allow her to lead him into a trap! He would first handle things so that he appeared to force information from her; so that he would be justified in seeming to believe her when she did talk....

"I doubt if the name means anything," Wentworth said softly. "Where to find the Falcon *does!* Lead me to him and you'll not only go free, but be paid for the information and paid well! Where can I find him?"

The Vixen rolled her head with its spreading crown of blue-black hair. "Oh, please—please believe me!" she begged. "I can find out, but I don't know now! Just let me make a telephone call!"

Wentworth laughed, lowered the point of the knife again, but allowed the Vixen to persuade him finally that she spoke the truth—that she would not know where to find the Falcon unless she made a telephone call. She described an elaborate system by which she could get in touch—an affair of relayed telephone calls.

"I'll have to give him a reason for getting in touch with him," she said swiftly. "Let me tell him that I'm leading you into a trap! That would be explanation he would believe!"

Wentworth nodded and the thought flashed across his brain that the Falcon would believe that because—because Dacey Hunt was the Falcon and knew the Spider had carried the Vixen into captivity! But he could not be sure. Iron Mike had been absent from the bit house this morning, and the man who had been in charge was one of those who had met the Falcon at the other aerie. It might not mean anything—or it might prove that Iron Mike at least was close to the Falcon. It might mean that Iron Mike was the Falcon himself!

From a compartment beneath the floor of the garage then, Wentworth removed a telephone—an instrument without a number which he had tapped into a line himself—and listened while the Vixen, with eagerness and desperation in her voice, put through her series of phone calls. He made a mental note of the system of identification she used and the Vixen smiled at him nervously.

"It's different every day," she said hesitantly. "If you had held me until tomorrow, I couldn't have reached him at all."

Wentworth made no answer directly. "When you get hold of the Falcon in person," he said flatly, "you may tell him that you have found out the Spider was behind the raid on Iron Mike's bit house."

The Vixen's eyes widened on his, then a soft smile moved her lips. "You are a greater man than the Falcon," she whispered. "Greater and more ruthless. I... like ruthless men!"

She waited for no answer, but turned to the phone again and this time, when the muted accents of the speaker at the other end of the wire reached Wentworth's ear, he knew that it was the Falcon who spoke! His cold hatred of the man who could wreak such slaughter for personal greed, shook Wentworth in that instant. If only he could strike over the telephone wires! He kept himself in rigid control.

Now if he played his cards exactly right he would end this reign of terror under the Silver Falcon!

CHAPTER 9
THE TRAP'S JAWS CLOSE!

WITH ACUTE attention, Wentworth listened to every intonation of the Vixen's voice, repeating the story he had instructed her to tell—that she had been the Spider's prisoner and that she had escaped because, she was sure, the Spider had deliberately loosened her bonds so that he could follow her to the aerie of the Falcon! Twice as she hurried through the streets, she had glimpsed a man on her trail. It would be easy, if the Falcon would make the arrangements, for her to lead the Spider into a trap!

Wentworth's lips thinned against his teeth. It was a good story, and just such a trick as he might be expected to use. But would the Falcon believe it, or would he guess at the truth? That was something over which Wentworth had no control.

He leaned close and heard the Falcon's sharp questions, the softened answers of the Vixen, as she explained all the details and said that the Spider had been boasting of framing the raid on Iron Mike's bit house. After she had spoken, the Falcon was silent for so long that Wentworth feared he had left the wire… then he began to speak again and with such cold and gloating venom that Wentworth felt his anger renewed bitterly.

"Rent a car," the Falcon directed, "and drive south on First Avenue to Nineteenth Street, then cross to South Street. Go straight to the warehouse—the doors will be open—and drive in fast. We'll take care of the rest! If we get the Spider, there'll be a special present for you, Vixen. Hurry!"

The Vixen hung up and swung toward Wentworth with a flushed face and her eyes half-closed secretively. "Was that all right?" she demanded.

"Perfect," Wentworth agreed quietly. "Now you will phone your friend Dacey Hunt and tell him exactly the same story—with *this* change. You will tell him the route you are going to follow, south on First, across on Nineteenth and so on to the warehouse, and when you have finished, you will hang up without waiting for him to answer you, or to change your route. Understand?"

The girl's face went even whiter than it had been under the threat of the knife. Wentworth's eyes bored into hers. If Dacey Hunt was the Falcon, she would be revealing herself as a traitor by that phone call.

"I can't," she whispered. "Oh, God, I can't! I would be betraying him to the police and… You don't know Martin Wolf! He would torture me to death, and he'd take a week doing it!"

Wentworth smiled thinly. "Aren't you overlooking the fact that you've already betrayed the Falcon… to me? Or did you use some code words in talking to the Falcon so that he would know it was just a trick?"

The Vixen had her shoulders against the wall of the garage and she was trembling and hate was in her eyes again. "You know why I made that phone call," she whispered, "and you know that I expect you to fail, to be killed by the Falcon! I used no code words, but with the Falcon it wouldn't be necessary! But the police…."

"The commissioner of police," Wentworth corrected. "Your

very good friend, Dacey Hunt, who looks so much like the Falcon! You will phone him now! Afterwards, you and I will do precisely what the Falcon ordered... with this minor difference. Instead of following you in another car, I will be right with you, crouching on the floor where I can't be seen. Do you understand? And a gun will be in my hand and its muzzle will be pointed somewhere in the middle of your lovely body. It is a large gun and it fires rather unnecessarily large bits of lead. If anything should happen to me, or if you should attempt to betray me... You understand, don't you, Vixen? Now, you will make *this* phone call!"

Wentworth was under no delusions about the Falcon. The minute description of the route the Vixen was to follow was a sufficient tip-off. The warehouse destination was a blind, perhaps to the Vixen; certainly for the Spider in case he should over-hear the conversation. *"Across Nineteenth Street to South."* Those precise directions could mean only one thing. Somewhere along the route, not in the warehouse, the trap for the Spider would be sprung. But the Falcon would be looking for the Spider in a car trailing the Vixen, and in the auto that followed her would be... the police!

The bitterly ominous smile clung to Wentworth's lips as he flung on cape and broad-brimmed hat and thrust the Vixen behind the wheel of his own car; took his position on the floor. When the police guns cut loose on the Falcon's raiders, the Spider would return to the attack. He did not think the Falcon would escape this time!

Yes, the Spider's smile hinted of triumph ahead, but there was

a small nagging worry in the back of his mind. Apparently, the fact that he had been able to force the Vixen to phone Dacey Hunt, cleared Hunt of all suspicion as the Falcon. There was no question that her fear of the Falcon was greater than her terror of the Spider. He had succeeded with his torture threat because the Vixen had glimpsed a way to save herself and at the same time trap the Spider for this man she called Martin Wolf.

The crack of the shot was drowned out in the deep-throated-roar of the truck engine.

There could have been no such hope in connection with the call to Dacey Hunt. If he were the Falcon, he would know, without question, that the Vixen had betrayed him... and he would exact his certain penalty. One more possibility remained—that

Dacey Hunt and her Martin Wolf were one and the same man. But the Vixen did not know that fact!

BEHIND THE wheel, the Vixen stared down at Wentworth with her eyes increasingly dark in a white face. Her hands rested limply on the steering wheel and she waited for his order. How much, actually did she know? If only he could read the contents of that small tight box of bone that housed her brain... He shook his head slightly, flicked on the radio control. He must wait a few minutes more to make sure that the Falcon and the police were ready to spring their traps....

The whining signal of the police station sounded and then the announcer's voice, sharp and positive, sending radio cars to stations near, but not on the route the Falcon had outlined.

"Signal fifteen," the announcer finished which meant, "Hold yourself in readiness for further orders at that point!" Dacey Hunt, too, was weaving his net for the Spider! Well, he would catch another more vicious creature... if his plans were in earnest.

Wentworth moved a little, restlessly, aware of the Vixen's dark, fixed gaze. He flicked the radio dial, caught the words of a news broadcast....

"... and what is the Spider doing while this holocaust of murder sweeps over the city?" the announcer was demanding. "I'll tell you where *this* mountebank was! He was arranging for federal narcotic agents to seize a batch of *stolen* drugs! Important, yes. Its value was several hundred thousand dollars and it had been stolen during the night by a daring one-man raid upon federal headquarters itself. But it resulted in the arrest of only a few minor criminals, of a man known as Iron Mike…."

Wentworth's eyes tightened. So Iron Mike had been arrested! That closed the cases, didn't it? It meant without question that Dacey Hunt was guilty… and yet the Vixen had telephoned to him her own death warrant, if he was the Falcon! Wentworth swore under his breath. Was he entirely wrong? Was there some actual man named Martin Wolf who had no connection either with Iron Mike or with Dacey Hunt? Wentworth's nostrils thinned and there were hard little lumps of muscle along the lean line of his jaw. It did not matter now. In a few minutes, he would close with the Falcon in that identity. Afterward… His attention jerked sharply back to the radio announcer.

"… That, ladies and gentlemen, was what the Spider was doing while this new terror ran riot through the city, while a hundred and thirty-four human beings were slaughtered in Grand Central Terminal; while another ninety-seven were murdered during the looting of the Metropole Museum! The police were on the scene, forewarned by this same Spider, it is reported, but they were only lured to their death! They died by the dozens in the attempt to avert robbery of the world's greatest art museum. A vain attempt, for the loot they took there is valued by the millions!"

Wentworth's stunned thoughts reeled under the impact of that news. In spite of his blow which had corralled the killers to whom the Falcon had imparted his plan at the other aerie, the Falcon raided the museum; successfully completed the looting and was free when the Vixen called to plot the Spider's death!

God, he had been so sure, and he had failed so miserably! The announcer was right to condemn the Spider, but he had been certain that the Falcon's plans were destroyed; he had not dreamed that, so soon after the Grand Central raid, he would carry out his second attack scheduled for today. It had been part of Wentworth's plan that if he failed in the present sortie, he would take up his stand at the museum and keep watch. Too late; too late… Ninety-seven dead, many of them the police….

"Isn't it possible," the announcer went on, "to ask the question: Since the Spider's warning did no more than lure the police into *this* death trap, in which they died by the dozens under the blows of some mysterious weapon that crushed their skulls… Isn't it possible, I say, that this tip-off for a minor dope raid was no more than an alibi to prove the Spider was somewhere else during this slaughter? How do we know that the Spider himself is not the same man who, according to the Spider's tip-off, calls himself the Falcon?"

With a sweep of his hand, Wentworth knocked off the radio switch and the eyes he turned upward toward the Vixen held burning points of fire.

"Drive on," he said, with a quietness that was more terrible than any hoarse rage could have been. "Drive on, and see that you follow the Falcon's route to perfection. I'm in a hurry to… *meet* him again."

The Vixen's lips were twisted in mockery. "Certainly," she agreed. "I'll drive on. I, too, am looking forward to your meeting."

She fought the cold motor to life, threw the car into gear and sent it rocketing out into the street. Afterward, she drove more slowly, but the mocking smile lingered on her lips in spite of the Spider's ready gun. She could afford to smile. Why not? Hadn't the Falcon beaten the Spider on every major count? Hadn't he escaped with millions in loot? It was true that she drove the Spider into a trap of his own devising. Her smile answered that. She was sure the Falcon would triumph!

THE VIXEN drove carefully amid the traffic of First Avenue and the overhead roar of the elevated trains announced her passage of Twenty-third Street. Wentworth felt cold tension mounting within him. No doubt in his mind that Nineteenth Street had been appointed as the spot where the attack would take place. He flicked on the radio again, waiting for the police radio cars to be sent to the attack. There was no whining signal as yet. Only the singing, crackling meaningless sounds of static. Wentworth gripped his gun and waited.

The Vixen's face showed strain now. It was patent that she, too, guessed where the attack would take place. She could not know just what the Spider would do. His face gave no hint. His plans were simple enough. At the first shot, he would render the Vixen unconscious by a stiff-fingered jab to a certain nerve-center in the throat... then a flank attack upon the Falcon! If it failed, he would have the Vixen prisoner and could form fresh plans.

The car lurched into a left-hand turn, skittered across traffic to the blare of angry horns, and was rolling swiftly along Nineteenth Street. The Vixen swerved around a truck that towered hugely over the car....

The crack of the shot came from behind Wentworth, almost drowned out in the deep-throated roar of the truck engine. For Wentworth, it was only a faint sound, half-heard on the brink of unconsciousness. It seemed to him, he had heard, too, the tinny slam of the lead against the metal door, but all of it was confused. The blow of the bullet plowing into his back, had hurled him against the steering post, against the Vixen's knee. It ran weakness through him like molten fire so that his automatic weighed a hundred pounds, five hundred pounds and tore itself loose from his hand. All his body was relaxing.

Numbness followed fast on the heels of that punch in the back. He was trying desperately to pick up the automatic again, but his hand was a fumbling, wooden thing, and the fingers without feeling. He was aware dimly, too, of the Vixen's hands beating down upon his head. He slipped down on the floor, rolled a little. His eyes strained upward and something loomed against the lighted square of the window. He could make out only the fiery red of a man's head, a pale blank that was his face, and he heard deep, ringing laughter, the Falcon's laughter!

"So ends the Spider!" he rumbled. "Nice work, Vixen!"

And the Vixen's rush of words, "Police, Martin! There are police all around here! Hurry!"

In the last flickering moment of consciousness, Wentworth knew the bitter taste of failure in his mouth. The shot would scarcely be heard, and the police following the Vixen could not yet have turned the corner. Escape would be damnably easy... damnably. Wentworth's futile anger rose in his throat. It tasted like blood. It was… blood. Then blackness swooped down upon him….

THERE WAS a sense of utter unreality about the fact, but Wentworth knew presently that he was still alive and that he was stirring from the deep unconsciousness that had held him. There was utter quiet where before all had been furious tumult, and he struggled back to possession of his senses. He knew presently that he lay upon a bed in the whiteness of a hospital room; that there was no pain in him at all—and that his right wrist was handcuffed to the head of the bed. It was some time later that he discovered the lower part of his body was immovable in a plaster cast and that his legs were without feeling….

That was Wentworth's first awakening. When he revived again, more completely in control of his senses, he recognized the Vixen beside him and that was a source of shock. He had believed himself a hospital prisoner of the police, but if the Vixen were here… Suddenly, blindingly, he understood. He was at a sanitarium! Perhaps the same one in which Nita was held prisoner. Even though that fact also meant that he was a captive of the Falcon, hope soared dizzily within him. It lasted until he tried, tentatively, to move a leg and remembered the paralysis that gripped the lower half of his body, and the bullet that had struck him in the back.

Wentworth rolled his head toward the Vixen and his voice came out more strongly than he had expected. "That bullet," he said curtly. "It hit my spine?"

It was hard to keep his voice firm. Of all ghastly fates which hell might have in store for him, *this* was the worst. To be paralyzed by a bullet in his spine—a helpless cripple in the power of his enemies!

"It was close enough," the Vixen told him, her voice incurious, while a half-smile moved the richness of her lips. "The Falcon tried his hand at a bit of surgery. He thinks you would walk someday, if you were to live long enough. Not very well of course. Not as well as you used to. And there would be some shriveling of the legs. That's inevitable when nerves are severed."

Wentworth shut his lips thinly and by a powerful concentration of will kept his face expressionless. There was gloating in the Vixen's voice and he remembered she had tried to kill him. Well, she was driving a different kind of knife into his vitals now, and there was nothing he could do about it. Nothing at all... He told himself fiercely that the Vixen might be lying... but why should she lie? He was completely at the mercy of the Falcon and his men, paralyzed and with his right wrist handcuffed to the head of the bed... A thin smile twisted his mouth.

"Since the Falcon has gone to the trouble of... operating on me," he said harshly. "I gather there is still use, even for a crippled Spider."

The Vixen laughed, warmly, throatily. "Oh, yes, indeed!" she said. "Oh, I should certainly think so!" She was still laughing when she went out of the door, and Wentworth stared at the ceiling.

Suppose Nita were here? He could do nothing, absolutely nothing, to help her. In fact, his presence alive might be merely used as a weapon against her by the Falcon. He would be better dead. *She* would be better off if he were dead. Wentworth had known despair before this, but never such absolute dejection, such complete helplessness. Always before, there had been the hope that if he could escape immediate confinement, he would survive to crush the enemy. Escape... *for a paralyzed man?* Wentworth's head wrenched back and the horrible self-mockery of racking laughter shook him.

The laughter echoed; it seemed to echo, but there was a deeper happier note in the reverberation and Wentworth twisted his head about and peered toward the door. Filling the opening, his fiery head thrown back in mirth, stood the Falcon himself!

Wentworth strangled the half-mad sounds that were pouring from his throat. Crippled though he was, he could not allow this butcher to pierce his armor. He turned the laughter into words that were harshly forced out now between clenched teeth.

"You've bested me for the present, Falcon," he said quietly. "In the only way you could, of course. Do you always shoot your enemies in the back?"

The Falcon nodded amiably and crossed ponderously to the bedside. "Naturally. It's the only sensible way, my enemy. Only a fool runs more risks than are strictly necessary... Which reminds me. You still have a certain power, Spider—something to bargain with. There is the matter of your reputation."

Wentworth stared up at the powerfully hewn, brutal face of the Falcon and felt the cold anger creep again through his veins. This was the man who had slain scores of innocent persons to line his pockets with loot. This was... Dacey Hunt or Iron Mike? Damn it, he couldn't tell! But it didn't matter, did it? A paralyzed man can not even escape from his enemies. And he would not give the Falcon the satisfaction of allowing his hopes to be aroused. Any bargain the Falcon offered would be very much like a bullet in the back....

"A bargain," the Falcon nodded his huge head, "but we will talk of that presently. First, I have a bit of divertissement to offer you." With a sweep of his hand, the Falcon extinguished the room's one light, and then wheeled Wentworth's bed about so that he lay beside the window. He rolled his head, peered longingly out at the moon-brilliant stretch of dead lawn; at the gaunt black skeletons of leafless trees.

"That's quite right," the Falcon rumbled. "You see, one of my prisoners expects to escape tonight. The poor girl doesn't think I know about it."

WENTWORTH FELT his heart bound into his throat. Could this fiend mean that Nita... He wrenched his head furiously toward the Falcon, but the man was not even looking at him. He was peering out at the moonlit stretch of lawn and there, suddenly, a woman's figure slipped out of the shadows, darted toward the bulk of a dead tree. There was an outbuilding, apparently a garage for a roadway curved out from its opposite side, a hundred feet ahead, and it was toward this that the woman was making her way.

Wentworth strained his eyes frantically. Was it Nita? What villainy was the Falcon planning? It was hard to keep his voice locked in his throat, but as he watched the woman creeping silently toward the garage, he tried to force himself to clear thought. There was no reason why the Falcon should work some of his torture madness on Nita, especially since he had mentioned a bargain. No, he would keep Nita alive to… to bargain with.

But suppose this were Nita after all! There was a grace in the woman's carriage and a proudness of the head that was like the woman he loved, but… He still kept his teeth clamped hard together. If it were Nita and she went to her death, it was better that way! She could hope for no mercy from the Falcon, and the sooner death came… The Spider would not linger long behind her; this crippled, helpless Spider who was no more than a plaything for the Falcon now.…

Thus he reasoned, but there was something in his heart and in his mind that was not controlled by reason. With a sudden movement, he snatched a glass from the stand beside him and hurled it through the window and, at the same instant, he shouted a shrill and frantic warning at the woman.

"Run!" he cried. "Run! You're discovered! You're doomed.…"

For a moment, the woman stood frozen, staring up at the window, then she turned and fled toward the corner of the garage. Her arms went suddenly above her head, clutching it as if some frightful blow threatened. She was like that when she ducked from sight around the corner; when a shadow darted down out of the darkness of the sky and vanished, too, behind the garage.

The woman's scream lifted in the same instant. It was fright at first, but only for an instant; then it changed horribly to pain. It shrieked and sobbed with pain, with pleading words. For an instant, it would die, then soar out with some fresh access of agony, exactly as if she were being tortured, torn slowly.…

Wentworth's voice was hoarse in his throat. "In God's name, Falcon!" he whispered. "Do something! Stop that... *torture!*"

The Falcon chuckled, a deep rumbling sound. "Calm yourself, Spider," he said gently. "That was not Nita. But I promise you, Nita shall run the gauntlet, too, and shall fail, unless you bargain with me, Spider! Nita shall go free if you agree to my plan. If you refuse... If you refuse, Richard Wentworth, you shall lie here helpless while she, too, walks across the lawn. Only she shall fall a little sooner—where you can see her, in fact."

The screams were fainter. There were moans and still they spoke of incredible, fiendish pain. Wentworth's fists were knotted white and helplessly. His legs... but there was no feeling there.

"The bargain is this, Wentworth," the Falcon said. "You shall take the rap for my crimes, allow yourself to be killed on the scene of my newest raid tomorrow night. That is not much to ask of a crippled man is it? In return, I promise you that Nita shall live, shall go free. Otherwise...."

His voice died, and like a hideous punctuation of his threats, the woman's voice shuddered upward in one final, awful scream; shrilled upward in the pitiless vault of the heavens and thereafter was utterly still.

CHAPTER 10
HANDCUFF ALIBI

INTO THAT silence, the Falcon laughed once more, plainly with unaffected amusement—mirth over that poor woman tormented to death! He left Wentworth's room without further words; without even a demand that the Spider give his answer to the ultimatum. More than any other thing, that action spoke of his contempt for the crippled Spider. It said more plainly than any words that *this* was no bargain as he had stated. It was a warning that Wentworth would do well to give no trouble before he died at the prescribed time, else Nita would be required to pay the penalty of his rashness!

Long after the Falcon had left him, Wentworth lay rigid in the grip of heroic anger—cursing himself for his utter helplessness in the face of this fresh and mocking challenge from the Falcon. That poor woman... but she was only one of the many victims. Heaven alone knew how many innocent human beings had died during the time he had lain here in coma with a broken back....

For the first time, the full grimness and horror of his fate struck him and the bitter lines drew hard and deep about his mouth. What could he accomplish now? But what had he done before that fateful bullet had crushed him into paralytic helplessness? Nothing, Wentworth told himself angrily, nothing at all....

A new thought struck him and Wentworth admitted to himself that it was bred more of hope than logic. He conned it with a fresh eagerness. Surely, if the Falcon wanted to kill the Spider on the scene of his latest raid, no such elaborate show as this wanton murder was necessary? He could simply carry Wentworth to the spot and then kill him. So that, unless pure sadism had dictated the gesture there must be some other motive than that the Falcon had voiced!

But what reason could there possibly be? He shook his head… then his eyes whipped toward the door. The white-jacketed man was bringing in a tray of food. Impassively, he placed it at Wentworth's left where he could feed himself—but he did it in such a way that he kept well out of the range of that one free hand. Wentworth watched the man keenly, but other than a refusal to answer any questions, the man might have been an attendant in any normal sanitarium.

Wentworth waited until the attendant had gone and then addressed himself to his food. In spite of his confinement and the severe wound he had suffered, he found his appetite good, and the food had been nicely prepared and served. Wentworth had a forkful of a savory meat almost against his lips when an answer to his mental problem struck him. Hurriedly he replaced the food on his plate. Could the Falcon's demonstration of murder have been intended to distract his attention from the food!

Cautiously, he tasted a bit of the food but in his enlivened

· *NITA VAN SLOAN* ·

state of suspicion, he was unable to tell whether there actually was something wrong with it or whether he merely imagined that it had a peculiar taste. Now that his mind was alert, it came to him overwhelmingly that he was damnably strong and of good appetite for a man whose spine had been damaged by a bullet. Curiously, he ran a tentative hand across his face, finding it smooth shaven. It might not mean anything, of course, but it was strange that the Falcon would take so much trouble unless... unless the Falcon wanted to deceive him as to the amount of time that actually had elapsed since he had been shot! That meant....

A violent tremor shook Wentworth. To his fevered mind, his foray into logic could produce only one answer. Lapse of time could be important only if the Falcon wished him to think that he was much worse injured than actually was the case! *Was it possible that his back wasn't broken at all?* Oh, it was madness to hope. Madness. Yet the logic of his discoveries could not be denied, and there was a way in which an injury to the backbone could be simulated; a very simple way. It only required an injection, according to recently developed technique, of an anesthetic directly into the spinal cord.

WENTWORTH LAY and knotted his hands into trembling fists with the effort at calm consideration of the possibility. Damn it, everything seemed to confirm it. The absence of the excruciating pain that usually attended such an injury; his own strength; his shaven cheeks and, yes, the murder scene that had been staged for his benefit! For, if spinal anesthesia had been used, it would be necessary to renew it in preparation for his journey to be slain in the city. Hence there would be narcotics in the food to put him to sleep so that he would not know about the injection!

Hope swelled within Wentworth for the first time since his grim awakening. He went hurriedly to work to conceal a liberal portion of his food in the bed clothing, and hurled the drinks through the pane of glass he had previously broken. Even so soon he was forming a plan for escape and attack! The white-jacketed attendant had kept carefully out of his reach, but later on another man would come expecting to find a victim in narcotic coma. He would have to come close to the bed to make his injection; in fact he would have to bend over it, well within reach of Wentworth's unmanacled left arm....

That was the chance.

Despite the elation that vibrated through him, Wentworth was by no means sure that his deductions were right. He fancied that when the attendant returned for the tray, to find Wentworth apparently deep in a drugged sleep, there was apparently a flicker of satisfaction in the man's eyes, but he could not be certain. There was no way to test his hope-fostered theory except to wait for the man with the anesthetic needle... Wentworth had waited for sudden death and he had raced against catastrophe to save people he loved from slaughter, but never had he known minutes to pass so slowly.

In his fevered anxiety, he lost all absolute sense of time. He realized presently that he could not swear whether hours, or scanty minutes, had actually passed and he fought for self-control lest his sheer rigidity should betray his trickery. But so much depended on his success! It was not alone that, liberated, he might rescue Nita and remove forever the menace of the Falcon. There was the fact that the Falcon was planning some new frightful raid upon sources of wealth in New York City—a robbery which inevitably would mean the slaughter of fresh scores of innocents.

Time and weariness finally brought him the relaxation for which he strove and the whisper of silenced shoes in the corridor—the ultimate appearance of a white-jacketed man in the doorway—came almost with a sense of surprise. And then Wentworth perceived the big-barreled, long-needled syringe in the man's hand! In that instant, Wentworth knew that all his deductions had been correct. He was not crippled. He would live to fight... to triumph!

A shout of joy that he could scarcely suppress flooded into his throat—and he lay passive, limp. He breathed deeply in the simulation of drugged sleep. And the man plainly suspected nothing. He came toward the bed....

Wentworth lay flat on his back, his free left arm thrown above his head, his eyes half-open to observe the man with the hypodermic needle. Every muscle was relaxed, ready for the supreme effort... The attendant carelessly deposited the needle on the white stand to the left of the bed, impatiently jerked the covers aside and stooped over the bed. He slid both arms under Wentworth to heave him over on his face, exactly as Wentworth had expected. Wentworth's right hand clenched on the bars of the head of the bed and, for just a moment, he resisted the heave of the attendant with all his strength. Then he struck... subtly.

The man was bending low over the bed, straining his muscles to heave Wentworth over on his face. Wentworth suddenly rolled in the direction the man was heaving. At the same time, his left arm whipped down across the back of the man's neck. There could be only one result of the combined down-pull and roll to the right. The attendant pitched forward off-balance in a neat somersault across the bed.

It was a flying-mare executed from an entirely different position... but the attendant did not fly across the room to land on his back on the floor. That was because the Spider's arm, whipping down across his neck, became a headlock that bound the man's face firmly against Wentworth's chest. The man's body described a somersault; his head could not follow the arc. There was the beginning of a scream, strangled against Wentworth's chest, then a dull snap. The wrench of the descending body dragged Wentworth from the bed, left him dangling from his manacled wrist, his legs impotent upon the floor. But the attendant would not move again, not with a broken neck....

FRANTICALLY, WITH the strength of his arms, Wentworth dragged himself back into the bed, rearranged the covers. His left shoulder had been strained by the wrench of the man's somersault, but he scarcely felt that in the greater excitement. Had that muffled scream, the thud of the falling body been heard? He lay passive, waiting, the body out of sight behind the bed from anyone passing in the hall. Minutes dripped past torturously, and there was no further sound. Wentworth drew in a deep breath and set himself about his next task. By strenuous effort, he hauled the man's body nearer the bed and ran rapidly through his pockets. There were keys, but none to the handcuffs, a helmet-type head covering of red silk, some money. There was no weapon except a pocket knife....

Wentworth's hand closed thankfully on the knife. He twisted about and peered at the handcuff, set to work. It would have been an impossible task for any man who did not know the intricacies of the lock perfectly. It was awkward for the Spider to use his left hand and there was several ugly cuts on his wrist and hand before he achieved his purpose of inserting the thinnest blade

131

of the knife between the ratchet of the adjustable bracelet and the dog which held it in place. Fifteen minutes after the attendant had entered the room, Wentworth's hands were free. His hands, yes, but his legs....

Wentworth remembered now that he had felt a definite shock run through his legs when they struck the floor in his fight. There was a tingling in them that was like the prickling of restored circulation after it had been retarded by pressure. But how long would it be before he regained the ability to walk? Wentworth tried, without result, to move his toes, his foot. The perspiration had sprung out on his forehead, but his atrophied nerves would not respond. How long....

But, damn it, he could not delay. Impossible to conjecture how long it would be before the man he had killed would be missed. Surely, not much longer. The Spider could not wait....

With a half-formed plan in his mind, Wentworth rolled to the edge of the bed and planted his palms on the floor. He dragged his body forward and his useless legs thudded down. It *hurt!* Joyfully, Wentworth knew that it hurt, but he was still a long way from using his lower limbs. He had to hurry. Arms rigidly braced, his legs dragging, Wentworth crawled toward the hall door. He was without a weapon, yet he pressed on. It was madness... and it was magnificent.

But Wentworth was not wholly without plan. He had to travel seventy-five feet before he found what he sought... a wheelchair. It took the last dregs of his strength to heave himself into it. Afterward, he sat there with the sweat pouring from his body. He had envisioned something different from this—a search to free Nita, a charge on the Falcon himself, but he was confined to this one floor until his legs were able again, and that would be a long time, probably hours. It meant that he must be back in bed, apparently disabled, when the Falcon sent for him. The dead man must disappear....

Swiftly, Wentworth wheeled the chair into his room and dragged the dead man into his lap. He had only one hand with which to work the chair, after that. But he managed to get the needle, to pump the anesthetic it contained out the window and thrust the syringe into the dead man's pocket. Everything hinged now on speed. With the double burden, he rolled the chair to a window in another empty room, carefully surveyed the grounds below and then, deliberately headfirst, he spilled the dead man out to the ground below. He would be found, of course, but outside and with a fractured skull... which was the way in which men died when the shadows of the Falcon swooped down from the blackness of the sky!

Satisfied then that he had made the best possible disposal of the body, Wentworth wheeled out into the main corridor and sent his keen gaze questing along its walls. He had to reach a telephone and one over which he could talk without going through the sanitarium's switchboard. In most hospitals, he knew, there were public pay booths for the use of patients' visitors. If this place was similarly provided....

He raced his noiseless wheel chair along the corridor to an intersection and his lips parted in a grimly hopeful smile. There was a phone booth! Fortunately, he had retained money from the pockets of the man he had killed.

It was not easy to maneuver the wheel chair to such a position that, by leaning far forward, Wentworth could get his mouth within range of the phone's mouthpiece. There would be the jangle of bells when he dropped coins into the box. Fortunately, it was the type where money was not deposited until a connection was made. He hesitated for a moment and then, gambling on his guess that his own period of unconsciousness had lasted no more than forty-eight hours at the most, he put through a call to the home of his friend, Stanley Kirkpatrick.

There was an interminable wait while the line hummed and buzzed and Wentworth kept conning the hallways. If he were discovered… He must be sure to get his full message to Kirkpatrick.

"Deposit thirty-five cents, please," the operator instructed.

Wentworth winced at the jangle of the bells as the coins dropped, then a voice came over the wire. It was not Kirkpatrick speaking, but Wentworth recognized the tones instantly. Dr. Bradley was still on the job.

"Don't talk—*listen!*" Wentworth pushed out hurriedly, speaking in a low, but distinct voice. "This is Wentworth. The Falcon is planning a raid on a half dozen big banks in New York City during the night—about the after-theater hour, I believe. The police will be safe if they wear red hats. Damn it, I'm not joking! I know how those people are killed; what crushes their skulls. They'll be safe with red hats. Tell Kirkpatrick to issue the orders, I'm in a sanitarium. Where, I don't know. They've given me a spinal shot. How long will it take finally to wear off?"

Dr. Bradley gave him a blasphemous answer and demanded

truculently where he was, didn't wait for an answer. "I suppose you know this confounded Chinese has been holding a man and woman prisoner here for the last two days, and… All right, all right. I'll see about those red hats, but you can bet…."

Wentworth was about to fling a new impatient order at the doctor when his ears caught the distant sound of voices, a shout of alarm. He swore under his breath. "Have *this* call traced!" He ordered violently. "Nita is here, a prisoner like me. We're going to be killed! Get the police here, and…."

HE DARED not wait any longer. He was sure he could hear footsteps on the stairs. Violently, he thrust himself from the phone booth, whirled the chair and sent it flying along the corridor. At his doorway, he pulled it to a halt and heaved himself to the floor inside his room. A thrust sent the chair caroming away into a dark far corner of the hall, but the hardest part of his task remained. Somehow, he dragged himself across the floor toward the bed.

There could be no mistake about the footsteps now. They were in the corridor, hurrying toward his own door. He was an interminable distance from the bed and his shoulders ached with the strain. He reached his bed, dragged himself into it and jerked up the covers. His hands were filthy from palming the floor and he was wet with perspiration. Impossible to deceive anyone now by lying quietly in the bed… With dexterous fingers, he snapped the handcuff shut about his wrist again, flung himself to the floor and began to jerk savagely at the head of the bed. He began to curse hoarsely, threw himself about, and… The Falcon stood in the doorway!

135

Wentworth raved at him like a madman. "You lied to me!" he cried. "Lied to me! If my back were broken, I could have killed myself! My back is all right. My legs...."

The Falcon's eyes were narrowed and hard. "Yes, we shall find out about those legs," he said softly.

At his order two of his men strode into the room and threw Wentworth back on the bed, pinned him down there. The Falcon lighted a cigarette and stood at the foot of the bed, puffing rapidly.

Wentworth knew what was coming. The Falcon was about to apply a simple test to see whether the anesthetic actually had been administered—the test of pain. If Wentworth so much as quivered a muscle when that fiery cigarette-tip ground into his flesh, his strategy would be discovered, a fresh injection would be made—and he would be finished!

The cigarette moved slowly toward the tender flesh of his thigh....

Wentworth was glad that feeling was not fully restored to his lower body. Had it been, it was doubtful if even the Spider's iron control could have enabled him to withstand the pain without the slightest muscular spasm in reaction. He cursed the Falcon steadily, and somehow he did not wince—and the Falcon was satisfied. He stood erect, tossed aside the cigarette and permitted his brutal lips to twist in sardonic amusement.

"It causes me the utmost regret," he said mockingly, "that we cannot be together to the last, Spider. Unfortunately, I have other business to attend to, and I feel confident that I can trust my men to take care of matters for me."

Even while he spoke, the men were ripping off the useless cast that had been put about Wentworth's body. A slight twinge ran through the muscles of his back, no more than that and the Falcon laughed.

"Quite a remarkable affair, really," he said. "My bullet hit the buckle of your really marvelous tool kit and drove it into the flesh. I think the shock to your spinal column put you out, but the wound is slight. We'll improve on that, of course, when you are deposited in the bank these men are going to raid. And they'll be careful to shoot in the same spot!"

Without further words, the Falcon turned and strode from the room.

For an aching instant, Wentworth started to hurl himself upon the two men who were working over him, dressing him as if he were an infant. He did not. For all the pain that had racked him under the torture cigarette of the Falcon, his legs would not yet answer his bidding. It would be futile. He would bide his time....

But misery went with Wentworth as they threw him into a wheelchair and carried him to the waiting automobile below. His eyes went up longingly toward the dour brick walls with their blank, unlighted windows. Behind one of those, Nita might be looking down on him. And he could not help her. Aside from his physical disability, duty called him to New York. However dear to him, hers was only one life and many were sacrificed there. Many....

Wentworth mocked himself with the thought. Did he then think himself capable of overpowering his guards and defeating

Those men wore green helmets yet they were falling everywhere!

the plans of the Falcon? It was madness. According to what Dr. Bradley had said he might expect to recover the feeble use of his legs within another hour, but it would be much longer than that before he could hope to be himself again; to be able to fight!

Grimly, Wentworth clamped his jaw. Never before had any consideration prevented him from hurling himself against his foes, and it would not now! He would triumph....

DETERMINATION RODE with Wentworth through the cold and blustering night. No effort was made to prevent his seeing the country through which he was driven. The man on his right, younger than the rest—but with the dilated eyes, the thinly egoistic mouth of a pathological killer—laughed at him harshly.

"Look at him, Pete," he called across to the man wedged in on Wentworth's left. "Look at him! He thinks he's going to have a chance to come back here again! Some guys are dumb."

Pete scowled. "I'd like it better we kill him now," he said shortly. "This mug is tricky. Do you dare kill him now, Sammy?"

Sam's face held its hard smile. "Sure, I dare. But I ain't. I like to watch him squirm." He ground his gun muzzle into the hollow beneath Wentworth's ear. "Squirm, damn you!"

Wentworth quietly turned his head. There was no particular threat in the straight line of his lips and the light in his eyes was pitying.

Rage convulsed Sammy's face. "Damn you!" he raved. "You think you're going to get loose and bump me, don't you? Well, you won't. You..." He jerked back his gun and raked at Wentworth's face with the sight.

Wentworth moved his head an inch, but it was enough to dodge the gun muzzle. It was one of the two men in the front seat who intervened.

"Hold it, Sammy," the man snapped. "The Falcon says not to mark him up. He's supposed to look like the leader of the mob."

Sammy desisted, but throughout the ride Wentworth was conscious of the hatred of the man. He would take the first opportunity to kill, no question of that. As soon as they entered the bank… Wentworth turned his head away from Sammy and stared straight ahead. His legs… He could move his toes a little now. He lowered his lids over his keen eyes to hide the exultation that blazed there. His crippled body might be ready in time, and meantime his mind was not impaired.

"It seems a little curious to me," he said mildly above the bluster of the wind that punched at the closed car. "Just a little curious that the Falcon should not accompany you on the most important raid of all. Doesn't the reason intrigue you at all?"

The man on the front seat beside the driver twisted about and put his contemptuous eyes on the Spider's face. This plainly was the leader of this particular group. "Now, what you trying to pull?" he demanded harshly.

"Leave me clip him, Bowler, just once," Sammy whispered his plea.

The leader, Bowler, did not answer. Wentworth smiled slightly into his intent regard. These men had no honor. Betrayal was a frequent experience in their lives and if they resisted the urge in themselves it was only out of fear of a stronger leader. It would not be hard to arouse their suspicions. And Wentworth had a trump to play… if Kirkpatrick had succeeded in conforming with the telephone message he had sent.

"I'll tell you why the Falcon didn't come," he said softly. "It was because the Falcon is finished with you. He's sending you to New York to die!"

The Bowler snarled and slapped the back of his knotted fist across Wentworth's mouth. "Don't think you can come that stuff with us!" he raged. "We're on to your tricks!"

"Please, Bowler!" whispered Sammy.

Wentworth shrugged and leaned back carelessly in the seat. "I warned you," he said quietly. "You'll learn the truth when you reach New York… when you see the police."

Bowler's eyes narrowed, but he only swore and faced straight ahead again. Wentworth hid his own smile and was content. He had planted the seed in fertile ground and it would take a while to germinate. He glanced carefully about him again. A roadside sign flicked into the headlights: *U.S. 202.* He knew where he was now! Let him once smash up this night's attack and he would race back to the sanitarium, destroy the Falcon, rescue Nita….

His jaw set grimly. He knew the slim chance he had of bare survival in the next few hours; yet he could confidently project such a plan! Resolutely, he refused to acknowledge its improbability. He had come through worse spots than this. That was what he tried to tell himself, and thrust from his mind the fact that he had no weapons and that his legs were… crippled.

Suddenly, Bowler whipped about on the front seat, "What the hell do you mean, wait until we see the police?" he demanded.

Wentworth smiled but did not answer. He was conscious of

the stares of Sammy and Pete now shuttling from his own face to the scowl of their leader. Sammy gouged his gun muzzle into Wentworth's side.

"Answer him, damn you!" he ordered.

"Look, Spider..." Bowler began.

Wentworth shrugged. "All right, if you're ready to listen to reason," he said. "It isn't that I give a damn about whether you're killed or not, but I'm not ready yet to die myself. And when the Falcon's trap is sprung on you, I'll still be with you."

Bowler hunched up on the seat so that he could reach Wentworth and cocked his gun to strike him across the face. "Talk, damn you!" he snarled.

"You depend on the Falcon to eliminate the police, don't you?" Wentworth asked softly. "His... shadows dive down and kill them off. That makes your task dead easy. You only have to walk into the bank, blow hell out of the safe and walk off with the money. But suppose the police weren't killed?"

Bowler snorted derisively. "Hell, they'll be smacked down like nine-pins! One, two, three, like that. They can't help being killed! Just let one of them poke his head out...."

Wentworth laughed, but made no other response. Fighting with words against death, against massacre... Bowler's glare was murderous. "It's a trick, that's what it is. The Falcon warned us to *look* out for your tricks. We ought to bump you right now before you talk any more."

"A swell idea," Wentworth acknowledged. "Then, in a few minutes more, you'll be killed and there'll be nobody to split the profits with the Falcon. He hasn't paid you off yet, has he?

Told you it would take time to realize on the stuff you'd stolen for him."

"You know too much," Bowler said flatly.

Sammy and Pete were scowling, but they didn't speak. The driver twisted his face around for a quick look at Wentworth, then turned back to the road. His shoulders were a little hunched and there was a frown between his eyes.

"Out with it!" Bowler snapped. "You talk, or I'll bump you right now!"

Wentworth held his peace for a full minute before he began to talk. When he did, he pushed out words rapidly. "You say, the police will be killed as soon as they stick their heads out? That's what has happened, in the past. But you men haven't been killed. You've had protection, haven't you? You wore red helmets."

"Cripes!" Bowler whispered. "Cripes! You mean the Falcon tipped them off! You mean they'll wear…" Suddenly, he began to laugh. Sammy and Pete threw back their heads and laughed, too, and the worry left the driver's face, reflected in the rear-vision mirror. It was apparently a great joke. "Maybe he did," Bowler howled. "Geez, wouldn't that be a swell joke? Maybe he did tip them off to wear red hats!" He doubled up with mirth.

Wentworth felt coldness run through his body, a coldness that was the apprehension of despair. God, had he erred? But, damn it, the men had worn red helmets in the previous raid and the attendant whom he had killed at the sanitarium had a helmet of red silk in his pocket… Yet there could be no mistake that the laughter of these four men was genuine! Suppose… suppose the Falcon had *changed the color!*

Something like a groan forced itself up into Wentworth's throat, but he bit it back. He forced himself to laugh. "Now will you believe me?" he demanded. "The Falcon changed the color for you, didn't he? But the police will wear red hats. The police will be safe, but you... you have been betrayed by the Falcon! *The shadows will kill you!*"

It was a frantic effort, and it was his last. Unless he could persuade them within the next few minutes that he was telling the truth, that the Falcon had betrayed them, it would be too late. For within a few minutes, they would be racing through the city streets and they would see the police in their red helmets. They also, Wentworth knew with a sudden aching certainty, would see those police dead... slain by the Spider's own warning! It did not matter that they would have been killed anyway. He had advised that they wear the red helmets... and that fact would doom them.

The car rocked around a corner while Bowler stared with speculative eyes at Wentworth, and the driver yelped out words. "Look! Look, there's a cop in a red helmet... He's *dead!*"

CHAPTER 11
DEATH RIDES THE WIND

I T WAS defeat for Wentworth's strategy, but even as he saw the death of that plan he was forming another. It was this ability to shift his plans in mid-fight that made the Spider so dangerous an enemy to the Underworld and which had saved his life more than once. But now he was fighting for more than

145

his life, fighting to avert wholesale butchery... At the driver's call, the men in the car jerked their heads about to stare toward the spot where the policeman in the red helmet lay with his skull shattered. They turned... and the Spider, handcuffed though he was, flung himself upon them!

His hands closed on Sammy's gun, wrenched it about and pulled the trigger in the same movement. He threw himself sideways against the man, Pete, crowding his gun arm against the side of the car and the captured revolver spoke twice more. The second shot blew the driver forward over the wheel. He was dead, but his weight held the car on its course while his relaxing muscles loosed the accelerator. The sedan moved on at a crawl and Wentworth wrenched the gun about toward the last of the killers.

Pete had recovered from his shock of surprise. He pushed Wentworth away, and it was an easy task for there was no strength in the Spider's legs. He could not brace himself. Pete whipped out his gun in the same instant, jerked it into line... It was the Spider's gun that blasted first. At that close range, the bullet ripped upward through the killer's face and exploded through his skull. He was dead before he could pull the trigger... and the car was still rolling sluggishly down the middle of the street.

Wentworth's shaking hands, as he rapidly gathered up the guns of the men, proved how debilitated was his strength. He was needing now the energy of the food he had dared not eat. But he could not delay. He pushed himself up on still numb feet that nevertheless were stiff enough to hold him erect, and gripped the wheel with one hand. He maneuvered open the door then and tumbled the driver from his seat, dragged himself forward.

It was an incredibly difficult task, but he dared not stop the car, or allow it to stall. Once it was stationary, he would not be able to work the pedals with his feet, and he had frantic need of haste. If only he could get word to Kirkpatrick. Damn it, he could not even walk to a telephone!

The car had lurched over the curb and narrowly missed a lamp-post with Wentworth's final effort to reach the seat. He slid into place and managed to right the car, send it trundling on downtown. He saw another red-capped policeman, dead... With one hand, he began to search the body of Bowler and, presently, in the inside pocket, he found what he sought. It was a silken helmet and it was... *green*. His eyes flicked to the street and rapidly he reconstructed in his mind the terrain that lay ahead. A grim smile touched his lips. He might yet be able to phone through the warning!

Five minutes later, he found what he sought—a police box fastened to a lamp-post in the middle of a steep grade. He could stop the car with the emergency brake, start it again by its weight on the hill. He leaned from the seat and groped the box open, wasted no words when the headquarters man answered.

"This is the Spider," Wentworth said curtly. "I warned Kirkpatrick to put red helmets on his men to protect them from the Falcon's killers. I was wrong. The Falcon's men are wearing green helmets tonight. Relay that message to Kirkpatrick at once!

Damn it, man, every second you hesitate some of the police are being killed! Phone Kirkpatrick!"

Wentworth hung up and delayed for a moment there on the quiet grade of the street. There would be patrol cars here to investigate within a few minutes and it was necessary to furnish proof of the thing he had said. Rapidly, he laced the green silk helmet on the shattered head of Bowler and, from his vest pocket, he slipped the platinum cigarette lighter which the Falcon had restored so that he would not fail to be identified as the Spider. He ground its base upon the forehead of Bowler and let the man slip to the pavement.

Wentworth released the brake and, such was the steepness of the grade, the car began to trundle forward even in high gear. The engine caught... and the Spider was racing away—late for his appointment with death!

SIRENS WERE wailing, but if the killers of the Falcon once more used armored cars, the police would be helpless. So soon as the police left their own machines, they would be doomed by the swoop of Falcon's shadows. And they would be leaving their machines, confident that the red helmets would give them protection.

Wentworth groaned and tried to pump more speed out of his roaring car. He ignored lights, cut recklessly through traffic. Occasionally, some car would give chase, but Wentworth soon left them behind. He was on the west side highway within a few minutes of his ultimate goal.

His plan of campaign? Wentworth did not know precisely. It would depend on the setup when he reached the scene of the bank raids. But the green silk helmet he had strapped over his head would save him from the shadows. He had guns… and the Spider's aim was deadly. His legs would have to carry him.

Wentworth plunged down the last ramp of the elevated highway to the street, whirled eastward through the city. In a few minutes now, he would close with the killers. He would try to hold them until the police sent out fresh reserves in the protection of green helmets to smash the Falcon's forces, and then… and then he could race back to the sanitarium to settle with the Falcon! He skidded the car into Broadway, running through darkness now that was complete except for the slash of his powerful headlights.

There was the bank, and he was late for his rendezvous. Already, one armored car was lurching away. A group of green-helmeted killers debouched from the doorway!

His eyes widened in amazement and a startled oath leaped from his lips! Those men wore green helmets, yes, but they were falling under the assault of shadows! The black, swooping forms darted out of the night and those green-clad skulls of the killers were crushed. They were spilled, already dead, upon the pavement. Their guns blazed up into the darkness for moments, and then it was over.…

Wentworth barely wrenched his car aside in time to save it from collision with the armored truck. Through the windshield, he glimpsed the wild, frightened face of one of the Falcon's men. He was alone in the truck, and he was fleeing… fleeing in mortal terror of this thing he could not understand—*that the shadows*

*which had fought on his side through many raids suddenly had turned
on the men of the Falcon and was slaughtering them!*

For a mad moment, it seemed an incredible accident to Wentworth, and then in a white flash he grasped the full meaning of
the thing. When he had taunted these men he later had killed
with betrayal by the Falcon, he had spoken no more than the
truth! The Falcon had the loot he wanted and he had sent the
gang of criminals he was using to their certain death at the
hands of the police, and of his own killers from the sky! And the
police... Here, the police in red helmets went unscathed. They
were crouched behind barricades and their guns were pouring
leaden death into the windows of the banks. That was the ultimate proof. Police in red had been killed on the outskirts of the
city to lure the Falcon's men into this trap, but here the police
found their helmets ample protection. It was the green silks of
the criminals that drew the sudden death from the heavens!

Wentworth threw back his head and laughed wildly. He
wasn't needed here any longer, was he? A task yet remained to
be done! He must race back to the sanitarium, kill the Falcon...
On the point of whipping the car about, Wentworth checked.
This was madness. The Falcon would not wait for the survi-
vors of this ambush to return and take vengeance. He would
have vanished long ago, *vanished*... and Nita! What would have
happened to Nita!

Wentworth was driving blindly southward through the city's
streets, but everywhere the bank raids were abortive, thanks to
the red silks which the police wore and the fury of the Falcon's
shadow killers. He turned northward and, suddenly, he spotted

a long black limousine which he knew was Kirkpatrick's private car. Kirkpatrick used that machine instead of the one allotted to him by the police. It could not be Dacey Hunt; could not be… Of course, Kirkpatrick would drag himself from his sick bed to join in such a battle as this. He… he had been blind, blind! Wentworth struck himself on the forehead with a clenched fist. He knew now how he must find the Falcon.

With frantic haste, he ripped the green helmet from his head and flung the car forward, cut in sharply in front of Kirkpatrick's limousine!

"Kirk!" he cried "Don't shoot! It's Dick! Dick Wentworth!"

HE DRAGGED himself across the car and put his fumbling feet on the ground. The police chauffeur was staring at him wildly, gun in hand. But he held his fire at a sharp order from Kirkpatrick, who was leaning forward in the tonneau. Wentworth seized the side of the limousine, dragged his fumbling limbs along the ground. He could see another man beside Kirkpatrick now… Dr. Bradley. The door whipped open, and Wentworth dragged himself in, already talking.

"Quickly!" he snapped at Kirkpatrick. "Drive to your house! At once, damn it, or the Falcon will escape us again!"

Kirkpatrick was frowning, but he repeated the order slowly to his chauffeur. The limousine was wrenched backward around the sedan Wentworth had driven, lunged forward again.

"What madness is this, Dick?" he demanded, his voice harsh with anxiety. "You phoned me to put my men in red helmets. I do, and many of them are killed. The Spider phones me to use green helmets… and men wearing green helmets are killed by what means God alone knows, for I don't."

"There's no time, damn it!" Wentworth said sharply. "Tell me… those prisoners I ordered Lee Chang to hold at your home. They're still there?"

Kirkpatrick's face was still pale and drawn with his illness, but it was patent that he had no idea what Wentworth was talking about.

Wentworth whipped toward Dr. Bradley. "You didn't let them go?"

Bradley stirred grumpily in his seat. "Do you take me for a fool? Of course, I didn't. I don't know what the hell it's all about. Are you under the impression that Doctor Martin Wolf is the Falcon? I warn you, there's trouble ahead for you in this, Dick. Wolf is a fine surgeon, a specialist in nervous diseases and brain operations. And you've kept him a prisoner like a common felon, without allowing him to communicate with a lawyer…."

Wentworth cut him short impatiently. "But he's alive, Bradley? He was alive when you left?"

Bradley swore, "Are you crazy, Dick? Of course, he's alive."

Kirkpatrick's voice lacked its usual strength, but there was no mistaking its crisp irritation. "What in heaven's name goes on here?" he demanded. "Talk fast, Dick, or I'll countermand that order. My duty is back there where my men are fighting…."

Wentworth forced himself to calmness. "It's simple enough, and you don't need to worry about your men. The Falcons killers are fighting on your side tonight. Those damned shadows…."

"Do you mean to tell me," Kirkpatrick demanded incredulously, "that these things that kill from the sky, whatever they are, have intelligence? That the Falcon can direct them on which side to fight? Dick, are you mad?"

"Not at all," Wentworth shook his head, even while he leaned forward tautly, as if with his body, he would urge the car to greater speed. "Not at all. But even the birds of the air can be trained. Falcons—are trained to strike at different types of game. How much simpler it would be to train birds to strike... *at colors!*"

Kirkpatrick stirred impatiently. "I didn't know that birds could see at night," he said dryly, "and the Falcon makes rather a point of having everything in darkness. Furthermore, no bird smaller than an eagle could strike with enough force to break open a man's skull like a melon! And an eagle doesn't kill that way, with the closed fist as many of the falcons do. It seizes with its talons... Damn it, Dick, are you mad?"

Wentworth shook his head with a slight smile, but his mind was scarcely on what he was saying. Would they be in time to save Dr. Martin Wolf? Where, if they were too late, would they find the Falcon again? The Falcon and Nita... if she were still alive. His fists knotted at his side, but he forced words out.

"There are certain birds which prefer the dark," he said quietly. "Birds as large as eagles. They have never been trained for falconry because such hunting was always by day when the game was astir, but there is no reason to believe that they couldn't be trained. In fact, the Falcon did train... *owls.*"

"Owls also seize with their talons," Kirkpatrick said dryly. "Dick, use your head...."

Wentworth's mouth was grim. "Tonight, one of them did seize with its talons. It used beak and talons on a woman until the woman died! But don't forget, Kirk, that an owl strikes its prey with all its weight. It flies silently and dives from heights as swiftly as any falcon... at least the Great Northern Owl does. I have yet to see one of the Falcon's lively little pets, but I'm willing to stake my life on the fact that he has used these owls—*and encased their claws in a steel ball!*"

KIRKPATRICK DREW in a sharp breath and Bradley's face was a little pale. In both their minds was the picture that Wentworth had conjured with so simple words. A bird as large as an eagle, flying at night and seeing with perfect clarity and trained to strike at colors. It would dive from a great height and try to seize that color with its claws—only its claws would be encased in a steel ball!

Kirkpatrick whispered, "It's ghastly... Who in God's name is this Falcon? He shall die, if it's the last thing I do. Who is he, Dick?"

Wentworth whispered, "I don't know. One of his names is Doctor Martin Wolf, but he is not Wolf."

"He certainly isn't," Bradley said grimly.

"It's simple enough now," Wentworth went on softly. "I should have guessed long ago. The Vixen told me that Martin Wolf was one of his names, threw the information out gratuitously. The Falcon told me personally that Nita would be imprisoned in a madhouse. A doctor took charge of Kirkpatrick when he was stricken in headquarters—a Doctor Martin Wolf who 'happened' to be there. You see, it was all built up to prove that the Falcon was a physician, a nerve specialist. But when I was a prisoner and had been subjected to spinal anesthesia, so the Falcon thought, he tested the completeness of the anesthesia *by burning my leg with a cigarette!* Scarcely orthodox, eh, Bradley?"

Bradley swore under his breath. "Of course not. The proper method is—"

"I'm damned if I see what you're getting at, Dick," Kirkpatrick said harshly. "You say the Falcon proved he was a doctor and then proved he wasn't...."

"Exactly," Wentworth said quietly. "He wanted everyone to believe he was Martin Wolf. If we're lucky, we'll get there before Martin Wolf commits 'suicide' under the Falcon's guidance; before he leaves a note confessing that he was the Falcon, but has killed himself rather than submit to capture...."

"My God!" Kirkpatrick gasped. "Faster there, man!"

The machine was already rolling at top speed. All three men were sitting far forward on their seats now. Wentworth was still talking....

"We couldn't merely send the police, Kirk," he said. "You see that. This is our only chance to snare the Falcon. Once he accomplishes his purpose here... I did have suspicions of Dacey Hunt and of a bit-house proprietor named Iron Mike. But I cleared Dacey Hunt by getting the Vixen to phone headquarters after she had phoned the Falcon the same message. Had they been the same man, the Vixen would have been dead by now...."

"Unless," Kirkpatrick said shortly, "the Falcon had a use for her. I'm not satisfied about Hunt's conduct of my office. The mayor appointed him without consulting me!"

"I see," Wentworth said softly, "and Iron Mike had an alibi. He was arrested by the federal men and was in jail when I was face to face with the Falcon."

"That's out, too," Kirkpatrick put in. "They arrested a man who said he was Iron Mike. He wasn't at all. He wasn't anything like Iron Mike!"

WENTWORTH HAD his hand on the door handle and the limousine was slanting toward the curb. His left fist gripped an automatic. If they were too late… The car jerked to a halt, Wentworth punched open the door and—pitched forward on his face. His legs had given way under him. He swore and Bradley helped him to his feet. He stumbled along. A doorman met them and hurriedly supported Wentworth's other arm.

"Has anyone left Mr. Kirkpatrick's apartment?" Wentworth demanded sharply. "Since Mr. Kirkpatrick himself, I mean?"

The doorman stared at Wentworth in bewilderment. "There was a doctor, sir," he said. "A tall red headed man. He was angry. He came out with another man that looked a lot like him and the other man gave the name of Dacey Hunt!"

"Too late!" Wentworth swore. "Back to the car. Where does Wolf live, Bradley?"

"Wolf?" Bradley rumbled. "You mean Hunt, don't you?"

"Wolf, damn you!"

Bradley was helping Wentworth into the car, and muttered the address in a disgruntled tone. "Look here, Wentworth, you can't talk…."

Wentworth flung the address at the driver and once more the car leaped forward. Kirkpatrick was panting from the exertion.

He was still far from well. Bitterness raked through Wentworth. An ill man and a crippled man, and a doctor who knew nothing of physical violence or fighting. They were a poor contingent to trap the fiercest and most clever criminal he had encountered in a decade of battling the Underworld!

"Dacey Hunt," Kirkpatrick was saying. "But why Wolf's home?"

"Wolf didn't 'commit suicide' at your place, Kirk," Wentworth said swiftly. "It would be much better in his own home. Evidence of his guilt will be piled up there. Evidence...."

Wentworth's heart leaped. Perhaps Nita would be there, too. Nita... *dead*. Suddenly, he knew this was the Falcon's plan. He surged to his feet, braced himself and shouted in the driver's ear. The Falcon had a fifteen-minute start. Would he compel Wolf to pen a confession, or would that have been forged in advance? But Wentworth knew the answer. The Falcon would not waste time over so futile a gesture. Forgery, certainly. That cut down the time... But they were almost there.

The heavy limousine whirled the wrong way off Fifth Avenue and hammered on a long slant across the side-street. The doctors home was a three-story brick mansion with a white, colonial door at street level. There was a light in the office window....

"Straight at it!" Wentworth shouted.

The driver nodded. He gauged his speed carefully and the limousine lunged across the sidewalk, jammed the left front wheel into the white door. It crashed inward and, instantly, the car was backing. Wentworth flung himself out and, a moment later, the chauffeur was beside him, an arm under his shoulders.

Together, they plunged toward the short flight of steps leading upward. Ahead of them, an inside door flung open. Light slashed out into the hallway and in the opening stood a heavy-shouldered, red-headed man. The doctor? The Falcon?

Even as Wentworth stared, he saw the man's hand whip toward his pocket. The Spider's gun spat in the same instant, but the police chauffeur was reaching for a weapon, too. His arm had faltered around Wentworth and those crippled legs… The Spider's bullet went a little wild. It struck the gun wrist of the man in the door. He cursed, and the door whipped shut. Feet beat heavily up the stairway and Wentworth sent a bullet winging toward the sound, surged forward. He head a woman cry out and he knew the voice. Nita!

WENTWORTH SENT another bullet into the ceiling, trying to panic the Falcon into flight. He heard Nita's scream rise, heard her voice, angry. She was fighting, but the sounds were retreating… moving upward toward the roof! Wentworth reached the head of the steps and, twenty feet ahead, a gun blasted.

Wentworth went down on his face. Beside him, the chauffeur cursed in a hoarse, gasping voice, thudded to the floor.

Men's voices were echoing behind him. Kirkpatrick's footsteps were heavy on the stairs. He was weak from the poison of the Falcon. He could not arrive in time. The chauffeur, wounded. Bradley….

No, no, it was up to the Spider….

"Don't worry, Nita," he called softly, "I'm coming. The Falcon can't escape!"

Cold air whipped through the hallway and Wentworth hurled himself frantically forward. So far as he knew, there was no escape from the roof, but the Falcon would have figured that out. He would have arranged a method of escape from the house after he had slain Dr. Wolf and framed the suicide.

The hall seemed endless. Wentworth's legs would not, could not move fast. He dragged himself on stiffened arms, a gun in his fist tapping on the floor—thud... thud... thud. But the Falcon was already on the roof. The stairs... Wentworth hauled himself up the railing, hand over hand, back down.

"Don't run away, Falcon!" he panted out mockingly. "You wouldn't run away from a crippled man! Not one you wanted to kill as much as you do me, Falcon? Wait a little while, and you'll have a chance to put a bullet in me! You know I wouldn't shoot at Miss van Sloan. Can you hear me, Falcon?"

There was no answer, but Wentworth could hear the soft, quick thud of feet. The sound was stationary. Nita fighting, held off her feet by the Falcon's grip, gagged—but still fighting. The Falcon was waiting.

Wentworth lunged out on the roof, fell flat on his face as a gun lashed out at him from the darkness of an overshadowing building wall. He wriggled forward, flat down, while the gun spat again, again... The third bullet hammered into Wentworth's left shoulder, high up, gouging into the blade. It seemed to nail him down to the roof. He cried out in a hoarse, frightened voice, made it, shrill with feigned terror.

Would it work?

He could vaguely see the outline of the man now, back against the brick wall, Nita in front of him. He could see him, but not clearly enough to shoot. Not with Nita in front of him. A vagrant gleam of light plucked into the darkness and touched the man's head. It was green… protected in a green helmet.

Another bullet hammered at him, but Wentworth did not flinch. He had rested his right elbow on the roof and he was holding his straining lungs motionless for this one shot. It was a risky one, but there was that faint gleam of green. If he could put his bullet there Wentworth squeezed the trigger. Then he waited.

There was a hoarse curse, and suddenly Nita was running toward him. Wentworth saw the Falcon sway out from the wall on widely braced legs. His head was down, and now that vagrant beam of light showed another color than green. There was red there, the red of blood! But the bullet had not gone true. It had been the merest glancing blow. The Falcon was coming toward him, roaring out his angry challenge, gun ready….

Wentworth leveled his automatic and his lips drew out into a thin harsh line. Nita flung herself down beside him, and Wentworth squeezed the trigger. There was a hollow, metallic click— no more. A curse ripped from Wentworth's lips and… the Falcon laughed.

"You first, Spider!" he said harshly. "You first, and then the girl! You thought you could snare me, did you? Damn your insolence! You…."

The red of his blood shone on the side of his green helmet and out of the night sky, a shadow flitted. It slid down the smooth ramp of the air, wings half-spread, stooping from enormous heights to snatch at that spot of red as the Falcon had trained

160

it to do, as he had trained others to strike at blue, at green, at a multitude of colors. It was a race between the Falcon's anger, between his trigger-tightening finger and the shadow from above. To Wentworth, the blast of the gun seemed the concussion of the owl's strike. The Falcon's head jarred to the side at an impossible angle. His feet flew from the roof and his heavy body thudded down. His bullet... *missed!*

NITA'S ARMS were around Wentworth now, and she was dragging him back to the protection of the door. It was only a few feet. He slumped on the steps and peered upward into the face of the woman he loved.

"There's nothing more to worry about, Dick," she said softly. "Not now that he's gone. You see, I'm your alibi witness for the murder they framed on you. I saw them bring that body in. That was why they had to abduct me...."

Wentworth laughed, pulled her down to his kiss. As Nita said, there was nothing more to worry about. The Falcon's gang had been shattered by his own greedy treachery; the Falcon had died by one of the killers he had trained, and the murder charge....

From the foot of the steps, Kirkpatrick's anxious voice reached upward. "Dick!" he called. "Dick! Doctor Wolf is still alive. We've got the Falcon on his evidence. It's Dacey Hunt!"

Wentworth's voice was suddenly strong. "You're wrong, Kirk," he said quietly. "It was Iron Mike—a damned clever man. Don't lose sight of that. Would the Falcon, if he were Dacey Hunt, tell the doorman at your apartment house his real identity? No, just a cover-up. One of many. You see, we still don't know who Iron Mike was before he became the proprietor of a crook hideout."

With Nita's help, he pushed heavily to his feet. "How about a little hunting trip, Kirk?" he asked, and his tone was mocking. "No need even to leave New York. Just borrow a friend's penthouse and shoot at the owls...."

His arm was close about Nita and her eyes were warm on his. "I," she whispered, "can think of much better uses for a penthouse. Especially a terrace in the moonlight." She shuddered. "But not until those awful shadow-things are gone."

Wentworth laughed. "All except one," he said grimly. "I'm going to find the one who killed the Falcon... and give him a pension for life!"